SHINE ON: INVASION USA

WW2 Patrol Craft Series Book 2

DONOVAN D CORZO
Corzo Creations, LLC

Table of Contents

Dedicated to the love of my life Kam.

Many thanks to the Tuesday night crowd for letting me bend your ears.

To Shari, who gave me that pen and told me to go and write that novel. I did, and here they are.

Thanks to "The Book Rack and Liberty Books" staff for letting me hang out for inspiration and research.

To all my family and friends. Thanks for believing in me and for reading the many rough drafts.

To Karl, my friend for over 30 years and my unofficial editor. I appreciate your honesty and experience.

To the Beta Readers and many volunteers who helped me launch this series. You have my utmost thanks.

To "The Lads," you know who you are and have been an inspiration for "characters" in the series.

Other Titles by the Author

Traveller Role Playing Game Supplements:

100 Plots ISBN: E-Book: 978-1-958297-04-9

100 Rendezvous ISBN: E-Book: 978-1-958297-07-0

100 Alien Rendezvous ISBN: (in development)

100 Alien Plots ISBN: (in development)

100 Underworld Rendezvous ISBN: 978-1-958297-10-0

100 Cargos ISBN: (in development)

A Time to Shine E-Book ISBN: 978-1-958297-00-1[1]

A Time to Shine Paperback: ISBN: 978-1-958297-01-8[2]

A Time to Shine Hardcover: ISBN: 978-1-958297-02-5[3]

A Time to Shine Audiobook: ISBN: 978-1-958297-03-2[4]

<u>Forthcoming Novels set in WW2</u>

Shining Through Battles in the Pacific: ISBN: 978-1-958297-25-4

Up in the Clouds: ISBN:

Peace Reigns Through

The Wars End

Other Novels set in the Same Period

Tales from Lake Tillery (in development)

---

1. https://www.myidentifiers.com/title_registration?isbn=978-1-958297-00-1&icon_type=Assigned

2. https://www.myidentifiers.com/title_registration?isbn=978-1-958297-01-8&icon_type=Assigned

3. https://www.myidentifiers.com/title_registration?isbn=978-1-958297-02-5&icon_type=Assigned

4. https://www.myidentifiers.com/title_registration?isbn=978-1-958297-03-2&icon_type=Assigned

SHINE ON: INVASION USA

ISBN Hardback: 978-1-958297-09-4
ISBN Paperback: 978-1-958297-12-4
ISBN E-Book: 978-1-958297-06-3
ISBN Audiobook: 978-1-958297-13-1
Registered Trademark through Corzo Creations

My Team

Developmental Editor: Do a developmental edit on your book by Inkfilaments | Fiverr[1]

Editor: Be your no 1 romance, erotica beta reader, copy editor, proofreader by No1_scribbler | Fiverr[2]

Alpha Reader: Be your alpha reader by Jwolffrath | Fiverr[3]

Beta Reader: Betaread and edit your short story or chapter by Genniferulmen | Fiverr[4]

Marketing: Promote your kindle or ebook on my website by Emilyheart | Fiverr[5]

Cover Designer: Do amazon kdp book cover, kindle cover or ebook cover with 3d mockup by Aesthetic_adeel | Fiverr[6]

---

1.   https://www.fiverr.com/inkfilaments/get-your-fiction-book-editing-awesomeness?source=order_page_summary_gig_link_image&funnel=721f824e39af629c6ae226d2d5ddf93d

2.   https://www.fiverr.com/no1_scribbler/be-your-no-1-beta-reader-and-copy-editor-of-steamy-erotica?source=order_page_summary_gig_link_image&funnel=9d5c59fa187e617b1726a53711577e12

3.   https://www.fiverr.com/jwolffrath/be-your-alpha-reader?source=order_page_summary_gig_link_image&funnel=56c8a1113f7b3badffa047d1c1cbf978

4.   https://www.fiverr.com/genniferulmen/betaread-and-edit-your-short-story-or-chapter?source=order_page_summary_gig_link_image&funnel=e6b3c728c97b964d80add2b8c6ae045d

5.   https://www.fiverr.com/emilyheart/feature-your-book-on-my-nextbookplace-blog?source=order_page_summary_gig_link_image&funnel=e919e7f57aec041a8605a6d358916325

6.   https://www.fiverr.com/aesthetic_adeel/do-amazon-kdp-book-cover-kindle-cover-or-ebook-cover-with-3d-mockup?source=order_page_summary_gig_link_image&funnel=220110415fa4a19c981e66568253a2a0

Foreword

I have done ample research and will provide a bibliography of sources. I use basic manuals from the time and believe in giving credit where it is due. I have attempted to follow history closely and stay true to form, but my days may be off slightly. I have also tried to follow the military protocols and expectations. I have taken liberties with some subject matter because if I didn't, the protagonists would still be in college or training until the war is over. I am sure others are better than me and could quote minutiae on what I got wrong ad infinitum. To those people, I say, "Get a life and write your novel. It's a work of fiction."

The main reason I wrote this novel is that sometimes the truth is stranger than fiction. I remember talking to a player at a Gaming Convention, and we were playing Traveller. He told the ref that he had secreted away some cannons, and when the pirates attacked, he popped the turrets out from the cargo areas and started banging away. I asked him where he got the idea from, and he told me about the "Q" ships used in the Battle for the Atlantic. Later, I learned about the "Ghost Army" and incorporated these unconventional tactics into this work.

I hope you enjoy reading this and other subsequent novels in the series or set in the same period.

Note: This novel uses period dialogue, including racial slurs. They are spoken between persons, in films, on the radio, and written in mass media. If the truth of history offends you, don't read any further.

PC-234: Morning Watch
Battle of Aleutian Islands, June 3, 1942

"Helm, come about to bearing 191," called Daniel as he felt the wind whipping around the bridge on Patrol Craft 234.

The sea was calm, and the clouds were few, but he could see a mass of black storm clouds and felt the cold wind biting into his skin as the atmospheric pressure began to drop. The Patrol Craft was a 173 foot-long, 450-ton diesel-engine with a single 3-inch gun open to the elements on deck, depth charges, anti-submarine rocket launchers, a 40mm cannon, and three double-barreled autocannons. In essence, it resembled a smaller version of a destroyer. Its typical job consisted of convoy escort and anti-submarine warfare.

"191 Aye, aye, Captain," called the helmsman. Dressed in a Navy work uniform, he wore a soft collard chambray shirt with bell-bottom dungaree material pants, a navy-blue knitted belt, and a white cover.

"What do you think, skipper?" asked Waisner, a husky Scot from Salkehatchie, SC, who was his Executive Officer. They were dressed in Khaki Uniforms and had previously served on the USS Aberdeen in the Coral Sea, where the ship was hit, and all officers perished. Before the last Officer had died, he promoted Daniel to Warrant Officer with acting Captaincy and was told to "FIGHT THE SHIP!" Well, he did. He fought the fires, the enemy, the elements, and the sea. He got the crew to safety, then was whisked away to Pearl Harbor to return as a Lieutenant Junior Grade five months later with his ship, PC-234. When he was reunited with Waisner, he saw that he was promoted to Warrant Officer, and he proudly gave Daniel the congratulatory letter from Nimitz.

"I think we caught them with their pants down," Daniel said, looking through the captured Japanese Binoculars with a five-mile range.

"Time for some payback?"

"Indeed! Let's wake them up!!"

"The Cyclops is launching ready fighters." Waisner nodded to the Yeoman, who pipped it through the ship's PA system. "GENERAL QUARTERS!! GENERAL QUARTERS! This is not a drill; repeat, this is not a drill. All hands report to your battle stations. Lock down all watertight compartments and secure all loose items." The Klaxons rang out with an "AWHHOZZAH!" sound.

"Action Starboard! Planes on approach!" Daniel called, which meant that the men would form an ammunition train to feed the guns.

The men were timed, and they were both impressed. The crew was starting to come together as a team. It seemed such a shame that all of them might not live through this battle. But it was what they had trained for. His gunnery crews could man their battle stations in about twenty-five seconds. They had used the aircraft to tow airborne targets, and his teams had such excellent fire discipline that they could destroy the targets before other ships in the Task Force had a chance to target them.

"All stations report manned and ready! Here they come! Target Aircraft sighted bearing one eight zero position angle two five," said Waisner, and they all heard the distinct sound of the Zeros engine. It had a high-pitched whine, turning into a deep rumble and roar as it flew overhead with the pinging of lead as they strafed the ship.

"Barrage Fire! Take dive attack sectors!" Daniel called out in a crisp and steady voice. His men shot back rapid fire using a pre-calculated fixed range, and the guns elevated sixty degrees so that when a target continued its course at the same speed, they would pass right through it. These devastating interlocking fields of fire they had established made short work of the Zeros and downed two enemy planes within a minute. Not bad. But that was not their goal. They were running interference and making themselves a juicy target for the enemy. The real battle was raging elsewhere around Midway Island. Daniel's crew had to stay in the fight as they were part of a convoy of "Q" ships with trapdoors in the decks that concealed six 4-inch/50 caliber guns.

There was a double hedgehog launcher hidden in the bow, plus machine guns and seven K-guns which could throw depth charges to complete the Anti-Submarine-Warfare component. Their Patrol Craft was equipped with electronic countermeasures and radios with recordings on wire spools that made them appear to be more than they were. They even had sonar microphones called hydrophones that made pinging noises like a squadron of submarines, plus they had pulled two retired World War One Flattop Carriers into the scrum—the Cyclops and Jupiter. Training planes (wooden mockups) had been stationed on the deck to sell the appearance of being a Carrier Group.

It looked like the enemy was taking the bait. But he needed them to commit fully. They were the "Ghost Navy." Now to pull it off. The name was GRB-SCW 112, but the crew called this float the "Garbage Scow." Most ships were barely seaworthy.

"Cease Tracking," Daniel called out, and the order was relayed. The guns went silent, and the stations resumed their alert positions.

There was sporadic contact, which was okay with him since the weather obscured their size and disposition. The area was where the two ocean tides mixed the cold water from the Bering Sea clashed into the warm water from the Pacific, which created hefty winds and helped obscure them from the enemy, but it also worked both ways. They were far enough out to sea from their target that they shouldn't encounter any Maru: merchant vessels up-fitted to act like PT boats that generally carried a large-bore machine gun or two and several torpedoes.

But they might not have to worry about that or be unlucky enough to be spotted by surface vessels. For if they got too close, they could see through the ruse.

Daniel remembered right after the final tactical briefing and before leaving Pearl, Nimitz waylaid him and twelve Captains and adjourned to another meeting room. He had handed over packets, looking like the cat that had swallowed the canary and had a devilish smirk. Daniel had looked up, his eyes wide.

"Well...what do you think?"

Scanning through the mission brief quickly Daniel asked Nimitz, "Are you sure?"

"Yes."

"Any practical reason as to why?"

"Let's see. We know where they ought to be and where we want them to be. But that's not guaranteed. So, I want you all to assemble this little flotilla and get them to commit! I don't want a kerfuffle or even a brawl. I want you to appear to be larger than life and wounded. Give them such a target-rich environment that they can't help themselves."

"But sir. Some of these vessels are listed as unfit for combat and barely seaworthy," said Captain Anderhouse.

"You can do repairs underway. Just put minimal crews on them and put these inside the transport ship. Then release them, and you will be like a magician pulling a rabbit it of a hat. I know there are risks. But there are always risks. Plus, I've rolled two defunct flattops to your flotilla, with trainer planes on the deck. You will have at least twelve, if not eighteen, working airplanes. The Commodore will more than likely use them for surveillance. I want them to think that we are so desperate to use these, which are held together with spit and baling wire."

"But we are.", said Spearman.

Nimitz shrugged.

"That's devious! What's the casualty expectation?" asked Daniel.

"No more than 25%."

"I see. So, what's the rendezvous point?" asked Anderhouse.

"Dutch Harbor, Aleutian Islands."

Daniel smelled salt air and was pulled back from his reverie. Unfortunately, he also smelled diesel—lots of it in the wind. "Waisner," he called out.

"Yes, skipper?"

"We've got company. Roll out the barrels!"

The order was given, and the Transport ship heaved to and started to open its hull with a whine as the doors swung wide once they were close to a complete stop. The PT boats and a few damaged craft swarmed, taking their assigned places.

A lookout called "Kates on approach!" Which was a Nakajima B5N carrier-based torpedo bomber from the Japanese Imperial Navy.

"Looks like we got their attention."

"Rodger that!"

"Tell the carriers to launch the remaining fighters!"

Carriers. What a laugh. The Jupiter was an old, converted Navy Fleet Collier with two launch catapults off each side and barely enough tarmac to arrest them once they landed. She had been built in 1919 and decommissioned in 1933 due to a force drawdown. Then, she was recommissioned and sent out to fight. In May, she was shot up by nine aircraft and was considered unrepairable since she was outclassed and ordered to be sent to the breakers. Her sister ship, Cyclops, was much worse for wear.

So, since she had over $300,000 worth of repairs, Nimitz decided that the least he could do was use her one last time in a desperate gamble to try and sucker punch the Japanese Imperial Navy. It was the ultimate "Up Yours!" maneuver. Now, they had the enemy right where they wanted them. But would it be enough? He had been given a merry band of misfits. Most of his crew were good at their jobs but played fast and loose with the rules. Over twenty had either been drawn from the brig or were on their way there. They were given a choice. Fight this one desperate battle and their records will be purged. If they died, they would receive full military honors, and their dependents would receive the service members' $10,000 life insurance payment. Not a bad deal. If they were all killed, the Navy still won because it would have gotten rid of most of its bad apples. Overall, 4500 men were staffing these craft, operating with less than skeleton crews. Typically, two thousand were on one aircraft carrier.

After the second pass of planes, Daniel received the order for even-numbered ships to light their burn barrels. These were red barrels with chopped-up tires, ignited with aviation fuel. This would create roiling smoke that would give away their position and make the enemy think the battle was going badly for them.

Looking through the glasses, he could see tiny black dots on the horizon. "Let's get cracking. Commence Fire," he yelled as all ships opened fire on the fast-approaching planes. The order of battle was for them to stage themselves into a pinwheel, while each carrier was to be at opposing ends of an inner circle with Jupiter as the Flagship. At the top was the Light Cruiser; the bottom had the Transport ship and a hospital ship dead center. All other assorted ships would run in a concentric circle, keeping distance, and overlapping fields of fire. Any stricken vessels would then rotate to the inward spiral for protection. The ring would continue to shrink as more and more ships were damaged. It worked on paper and in theory. It was just a circle of the wagon's defense instead of the prairie on the ocean. Now to put this plan into action.

All these moving parts reminded Daniel of the distinct features in a symphony. The PT boats were the string section, the Transport ship percussion; the destroyers were brass, the Carriers the wind section, and the Hospital ship tin phony. The Opera by Wagner was in his mind playing the Ride of the Valkyries. It felt weird to be sitting here on the command deck as a Lieutenant Junior Grade when he had been a gunner's mate, not five months prior. But that was war, and he knew that they were all expendable. He had hoped they could fight the enemy to a standstill at worst, but how much damage could they inflict? They had sixteen working planes, two of which were bombers, and they were about to be inundated with fighters. He had made sure that his men had practiced all of their maneuvers on the float and now he could only hope for the best and see how they fared against the enemy.

So far, they had only encountered air cover two by two. The first pair were scouts, and the bombers came in right behind, trying to take out the Carriers. Where was the rest of the group? Were these four lost?

In anticipation of the commotion that Nimitz had requested, they had overloaded every spare inch of the decks with anti-aircraft emplacements. The PT boats were sporting anti-tank rifles, and the four merchant vessels had five-inch guns. These were known as "Q" ships. Altogether he had quite an impressive amount of firepower, but would it be enough?

The TBS (Talk Between Ships) phone went off squawking: "Arthur Lake calling. Large swarm of aircraft Zeroes, Oscars, Val's, Judy's and Kates. Get ready!" Each enemy aircraft was assigned nicknames, with Zeroes being the fighter planes most servicemen went up against. The Oscar was a smaller, nimbler fighter with two 12.7 mm machine guns; they were constantly refined and even upgraded to a self-sealing fuel tank and armor to protect the pilot. They could also carry two 250-kilogram bombs. Kates was the torpedo bombers, and Val's were single-pilot dive bombers. Judy's were two-man dive bombers.

The Zeroes came in hard and fast, and the guns opened with a steady ACK! ACK! ACK! sound. Then the reports started pouring in from the flotilla. His command deck had several speakers set up to try and coordinate the mess. Everything was recorded on the wire spools for posterity and later review.

"Hammerhead six engaging," called a pilot.

"On your wing six, breaking right and windmilling." "Good approach, firing." (Loud machine gun noise). "Got him six; he's breaking up."

"Splash one."

Hammerhead four is down. They got HARRY!" said a nervous voice over the comm.

Daniel called over the TBS, "Keep it professional, people; rely on your training. We need reports!"

"Rodger sir, wilco! Hammerhead two he's coming in from the sun. Barrel roll left, and I'll line him up." The sound of firing guns followed.

"Hammerhead three, where are you? I can't shake this one. I—" There was only static. Daniel hung his head and spoke to Waisner. "Stay on this and coordinate with the pilots."

"They won't last two more minutes," said Waisner, exasperated.

"All we can do is fight and win or fight and die!" He had to turn his attention to the calls from the ships.

"Mantas one through five starting runs on Maru and one destroyer," came the call from the PT boats. They could hear the machine guns firing with their steady BBBRRRRTTTT, and then the BOOM! BOOM! BOOM! of the antitank rifles. There were several whooshing sounds as they launched torpedoes at their targets. A fireball erupted, and he heard cheers. But he knew that this fight was about to get expensive. He looked through the glasses. One of the PT boats was on fire, and the destroyers, Arthur Lake and Jean Laffite had bracketed the oncoming destroyer that was just out of support range from the convoy. The PT boats had softened it up, and the destroyers five-inch guns were pounding it to scrap. He heard a loud boom at the six-o clock position and saw one of the "Q" ships take a hit. But they were firing like madmen at the wave of fighters, and he saw several splashes into the sea.

"Dorian is lost," called a voice.

"Who is this?" Daniel asked over the TBS.

"Sorry, sir, Jean Lafitte here. The Dorian just went under."

"Was she hit?"

"Jean Lafitte here: No, sir, I don't think so. She just slid under the water." Daniel made a mental tally and realized he was down by four percent of manpower and twelve percent of ships between that and the PT boat. They were barely five minutes into the engagement.

Waisner threw a coffee cup, which shattered as he yelled, "SON OF A BITCH!"

Daniel called out, "BELAY THAT! What's going on?" he said, marching sternly over to Waisner, who just hung his head at the rebuke.

" Sorry, sir," he mumbled, "We just lost all the planes."

"Then go coordinate with the "Q" ships, and we just lost the Dorian"

"How many made it out?" Waisner asked, his face ashen.

"None, she just went under!" he said frankly, turning to announce, "Tighten up your screen, people. Close those gaps and get ready for the next wave."

His men fought bravely, and he watched the Salt Lake City CA-25, a Pensacola class cruiser nicknamed "Old Swayback", make a daring run at the Japanese Light Cruiser Tama with the PT boats harrowing it, making it jog left and right. The captain of "Old Swayback" called out over the TBS, "Here's where you separate the men from the boys. Make way, coming through!"

Meanwhile, Arthur Lake came in from the lee side and launched her depth charges high and at the oblique, which caused them to detonate in an airburst and tear into Tama's forward guns. It was followed up with a barrage of thirty-six hedgehogs. These were mortar rounds that were generally used in submarine warfare that packed thirty pounds of explosives in their warheads which were contact explosives that detonated when they hit any hard object. The entire forecastle was rent open, and fire slowly engulfed the ship. Two other explosions ripped into her rear, and the Tama cracked in half. Two pieces drifting apart and collapsed into the sea. He was now down by three ships as another PT boat succumbed to its wounds.

His order of battle was starting to look ragged as there had been a bulge when those seven ships went after the destroyer. So, Daniel called out, "All vessels report back to your positions on the line."

A yeoman called out, "Sir, we've managed to down twenty-five planes, five Kates, and the rest Zeroes!"

"Put it up on the board," he said tiredly as he downed a cup of coffee two hours cold.

The battle raged on, and they began to suffer from attrition. He couldn't get a read on how many he was fighting. Were they part of a larger taskforce spun off to deal with him? He wasn't sure.

Two aircraft made it through the screen and targeted his ship. "Helm, come about starboard 30 degrees," Daniel ordered.

"Starboard 30 degrees. Aye!" They fired the antiaircraft guns and then 40 mm when they got closer. This turned his ship hard left, putting it in a placement to attack the aircraft and eventually bracket it. They shot one to pieces and splashed into the sea, barely missing his ship. A dive bomber screamed in from above, but it was at a poor attack angle, and there was a quick two-way battle of gunnery. The main problem was that the only way to win was to blow the aircraft to smithereens and dodge the wreckage. Otherwise, they would just get hit with shrapnel.

"PORT SIDE TORPEDO BOMBER!" called a watchstander excitedly. He turned his attention and saw the plane coming in about forty feet above the water, and it was under his guns.

"HELM HARD LEEWARD!" yelled Daniel.

"HARD LEEWARD AYE!" the helmsman said as he frantically spun the wheel to the left.

"Come on, come on, come ON! ALL GUNS FIRE LOCALLY!! Direct fire to match parallax." Daniel said. "Rapid continuous fire!"

The ship groaned and turned to the left-leaning upwards at about a 15-degree pitch. It was enough to give the gunners the correct angle to hit the aircraft, and it exploded. They might have hit the gas tank or the torpedo. But they didn't have time to think about it as they had planes coming in from every angle. Daniel saw another plane go down, and its ruptured gas tank spewed a lethal arc of combustible fuel all over the Jupiter. The Japs had enough planes through the screen and were targeting the Carriers. Another dive bomber climbed to 1500 feet and started its run when a 30mm gun mount from LSC-512 took it out. Unfortunately, the engine struck amidships, killing many men. But the support ship had effectively screened the carrier.

He saw a 500-pound bomb hit 512 and slam into the rudder; now, they couldn't steer. He was too far away to help and too busy to fall out of position in the order of battle.

Suddenly, he heard a crackle of static on the planes squawk box. "Blue Squadron Leader is coming in high to assist. Protect the Carriers."

"Rodger that," called Wiesner, "How many in your group?"

"Just four left, sir. We've been taking a pounding. They've attacked Dutch Harbor. We were out on patrol and found this fracas. We will cover but need to land and rearm and refuel. We can't raise the carriers."

"We will signal it over," said Daniel as he nodded to his signalmen, who ran up flags. They relayed the request, and landings were approved.

Five minutes later, two planes touched down on the decks of the Cyclops while the other two performed a combat air patrol to cover them. The Jupiter was fighting the fires on the top deck and couldn't do anything else.

"Torpedo in the water, starboard side!" called a watchstander.

"Range?"

"Half a mile?"

"Sonar, get me a bearing."

"342."

"Rodger that, Helm. Come about to 342 smartly."

"342 smartly, AYE sir!"

"Combing it," said Waisner, which meant they had turned to bring the ship to parallel the torpedo. This presented a much smaller target.

"Fire depth charges high and low on 275."

"Firing high and low, AYE!" called the weapons officer.

A few seconds later, loud explosions blasted the water off the starboard side. Daniel looked through the binoculars and didn't see an oil slick or debris.

He heard more airplanes approaching the flotilla and called out. "Waisner, tell those planes that they must take off now!"

"Rodger, that skipper!"

A few seconds later, he could see them roaring off the flattop. "We only got half a load, but it's better than none," called Blue Squadron Leader. The two planes flying the cap then landed, as well. Hopefully, they could get more ammo and fuel in the next three minutes. The worst thing that could happen was they ended up on the deck when the carrier was hit. Twenty more enemy planes entered the theater of operations and went to work harrying the defenders. His group was making short work of the rookie pilots. But the remaining half were pros and started attack runs in earnest.

Daniel called over to the Combat Information Center, the CIC, to ask how many they were facing.

"Well, skipper, overall, we are looking at two aircraft carriers, assorted cruisers, a few destroyers, a dozen support ships, and maybe half a dozen submarines."

"Well, where are they?"

"Strung out over a five-mile path. The volcanic ash that is spewing constantly along this island chain is playing merry hell with our equipment and likewise for them. The tides and currents push us all over the place. We have updated maps and sounding of the local area. They might not."

The remaining planes had refueled and were airborne again. They chased off the attackers and ran down any stragglers. But now they were out of ammunition as they only had enough time to get forty-five seconds of ammo, about 500 rounds. So, they did their best and started runs with barely enough ammo for a minute's combat.

To conserve it, they fired their guns individually. They harassed the enemy and forced them into turns which ran them into the waiting guns. Two hours later, the engagement was over, and they were told to turn to and head for Dutch Harbor. Two planes were left, and they landed on the Cyclops. He coordinated with a support ship to try and rescue anyone left in the water as they could freeze to death in minutes. None were saved.

"Report Casualties!" Daniel ordered, and they came pouring in from all over the ship. Mostly just bumps and bruises, a snapped wrist or two but nothing major.

"Secure from General Quarters. Set Condition One. The smoking lamp is lit."

Several hours later, they pulled into the harbor and surveyed the damage. Dutch Harbor had taken a pounding. Bomb craters pitted the ground, and flames rose from the fuel dumps; crews doused them with foam. They were glad the island had good anchorage and pulled into a mooring area.

He called out the commands to park the ship and told the crew to lower the gig. He ordered the men to be fed and turned the ship over to a junior officer while he and Waisner went ashore to turn in their reports and see what orders would follow.

Dutch Harbor, Aleutian Islands
Midwatch June 4, 1942

The gig pulled up to the temporary dock, which was little more than a bunch of fuel barrels strung together with planking tied in place. Daniel called it 'Crude but effective!'

He and Waisner disembarked, and they were directed to the radio station. They noticed a bar called "Blackies" and a sign was outside bragging about fifty-cent whiskey shots. A sign was next to it declaring the night's movie with admission prices as fifteen cents for military personnel and thirty-five cents for civilians.

He surveyed the area and noticed that the vegetation was a russet color but seemed drained and stretched too thin. The ground was volcanic ash and mixed with the local flora became a very thick concoction of mud. There were puddles of water everywhere, and in the far background, he could see giant cones of active volcanoes as they spewed clouds of steam. The wind bit through his uniform, and he told himself to remember his trench coat next time. This place was as lonely as the moon's surface, and its only value seemed to be strategic.

He was glad that the gamble from Nimitz had paid off as they seemed to arrive in the nick of time. They entered the building and reported it to the Commander of the Base. He thanked them for their support and asked what they could spare. Daniel agreed to some replacement parts and assorted foodstuffs that were long-term storage and had to be rotated anyway. He knew his crew would grumble a bit, but all he had to do to shut it down was for them to look out and see the destruction. So, they ate cold sandwiches now and again.

These men survived off powdered eggs, canned beef, tomatoes, peanut butter, biscuits, and coffee. No fresh meat or vegetables. They had also requested that he cut up the tin cans, flatten them out, and deliver them with the rest of the supplies. It turns out they were using them as patches for the aircraft.

He coordinated the times for the exchange with the base, and then they returned to the ship. The Commodore set up work parties and semi-liberty privileges for movie night; they would see what they had in their libraries and try to get some new material. He knew his ship had a documentary on the construction of the Empire State Building and a New York City tour.

He was ordered to anchor at the mouth of the harbor and keep watch for any enemy, especially submarines, and protect the Hospital ship. They came on-station an hour later. The crew had been fed, and ammunition replenished. All repairs completed; all work done. They would need to be extra vigilant as complacency could get them killed. He turned Command over to the Officer of the day and retired with Waisner to the wardroom. They only had five officers on this vessel; it was simply a table for eight built into the bulkhead. The galley had a small flattop, frying unit, steam trays, and a simple passthrough. He could smell the burgers and bacon cooking and his mouth watered. He didn't remember the last time he had eaten, so he looked forward to it.

A mess steward brought a pitcher of iced tea and two glasses. They nodded thanks, and Daniel asked, "Can the cook put an over-easy egg on the burger?"

"Certainly, sir."

"I can hear a 'but' coming."

"Well, sir, we generally save those types of eggs for baking cakes."

"I know that since I'm the one that provisioned the ship. I allocated a few extra just for this occasion," he said with an air of finality.

"Rodger that. Coming up," said a disembodied voice from the galley. The meal arrived a few minutes later, and the plates contained two hamburger sandwiches, each with lettuce, tomato, onion, mayo, and ketchup. Pickles were on the side, as well as mustard. The piece de resistance was the wedges of fresh-cut fries and the over-easy eggs on top of them.

Waisner and Daniel bowed their heads in prayer, giving simple thanks for surviving another day. The mess attendant also respectfully followed suit. Then they dug in; chewing was the only sound heard for the next several minutes as they demolished the burgers. The egg yolks broke and were running down their hands. The mess steward was aghast and promptly brought in finger bowls with hot towels. They finished up and wiped their hands clean.

Then, they started in on the pickles. These were small gherkins, very sweet, and snapped when you bit into them. So, he and Waisner laughed as they polished them off. Next, he asked for hot sauce and started dunking his fries. The dessert was canned peaches with ice cream, followed by coffee. The cutlery was simple, and the cups were the same as the rest of the ship, unlike the Aircraft Carrier he had been on when he was first brought up to Warrant.

Now that dinner was out of the way, they could prepare the after-action reports and see to the information required for the ship to run smoothly. There were duty rosters and crew rotations to go over. All of which could be changed if they went to Action Stations. This ship was a piece of machinery, and she needed to be maintained at regular intervals. They decided to send a work party of twelve ashore the first chance they got with a new movie delivered to the theater, swapping it out for one they hadn't seen yet. The party were then to place themselves at the disposal of the 'officer' of the day. Once they returned, they would set up for a movie night of their own in the main galley.

They were scheduled for a day of rest and then go on patrol the following day. They were to perform a picket duty for 200 nautical miles, sweeping up and down the coast and coordinating with aerial units and other ships of the line to pinpoint the enemy's location. He was briefed that they were ramping up to build a base on the island of Avak. Overall, the combined might of the aircraft and flotilla had taken out two troop-filled transports, three heavy cruisers, two destroyers, and one aircraft carrier. But they still didn't know where the rest of that fleet went. Now the hunt was to begin in earnest.

Once the paperwork was done, he retired to his quarters and took a shower. He did not have the luxury he did on land or on the destroyer. Hot water was at a premium, so he had to turn on the taps and, walk forward, turn off the taps. Then soap himself up and turn on the tap, rinsing off quickly. He was also brushing his teeth at the same time. In these close confines, efficiency was the best way to go.

Once evening ablutions were complete, he sat at his small desk and composed a note to his wife.

Vmail Postcard: From Daniel Core

My Darling,

How are things? The moon here is very bright and reminds me of our times on the porch at home. Whenever I look at that big white disk, I think of you. I am eating well and getting enough sleep. How are the children, and did Miranda ever learn to drive the "BEAST"?

With much Love,

Danny

He couldn't add any more, and it was far easier to send a postcard than a letter. She thought he was cross with her the first time he had sent a short note. So, when he returned home, he explained to her that all mail was censored and there was only so much he could tell her. They didn't want the enemy reading their mail, so this was the best option. She finally understood but seemed disappointed. He told her, "Just pay attention to the details."

"Like what?"

"Dear Kim-Yee, I miss you; Love Danny," he said thoughtfully.

"But that's absurd."

"Doesn't mean it's not true. It's what we must sacrifice if we ever win this war. Just get used to it. You can write to me whatever you want. But if they think anything is sensitive or just bad news, they will cover it up with those ugly black sensor lines."

He finished writing and placed it in the outgoing slot.

The following day they were underway on their picket duty. They got a few minor pings but couldn't determine if it was a submarine or a pod of whales. But he had the men assume action stations and gave the command for "Torpedo Defense." All antisubmarine gun crews and control parties reported to their stations on the double. When all manned and ready, the Engineering and Damage Control Stations were alerted the enemy was playing quiet, so he and his men kept a watchful eye. He heard planes overhead but wasn't sure who they were since they were above the cloud cover. They sounded like a few bombers and a Catalina PBY, but he couldn't be sure from their noise since they were so high up. But since they were headed west, he was assured they were on their way to bomb the island of Kiska. That was where the Japs had retreated to as far as they could ascertain. The runs had been continuous with sorties starting at dawn and then launched every hour on the hour for twenty hours straight. Many crews landed, refueled, rearmed, and went back up.

So far, he was aware that two pilots had been lost due to either bad weather, poor visibility, or no fuel. He kept an eye out for downed planes but didn't see any. It was strange that even though he had never heard of this place before, he and his comrades in arms had been defending it with everything they had. This was a part of America. The defenders of Dutch Harbor had paid a dear price with forty-three dead, fifty wounded, fourteen aircraft, and one barracks ship destroyed. They badly needed the spare supplies they could scrounge from the flotilla and were thankful for the two Carriers parked outside the harbor. This would allow them greater flexibility for the air war against the enemy. Not to mention that even though they were old, they had spare parts and machine shops so they could mill whatever they required. Plus, they could save on fuel and flight time.

The soldiers at Fort Mears were now living out of large conical tents, but at least the mess hall, which could feed 500 and doubled as the theater, was intact. The base was ringed with anti-aircraft and artillery batteries manned by the Arkansas National Guard, and they had been on station for roughly four months. The Japanese had planned their attacks well and tried to extend their defensive perimeter and establish a foothold. When the attack came, the defenders scrambled to their stations and began fighting off the assault of 12 Zeroes, 10 Kates, and 12 Val's. They began strafing runs against the guns and set two barracks ablaze. They also targeted the Northwestern, a transport ship that was beached and used as a barracks for the civilian contractors. A hospital wing was damaged, and two merchant ships had been in the harbor.

FLASH TRAFFIC
June 15th, Aleutian Islands, Alaska

PC-234 was out on patrol when Flash traffic was sent to the radio room, and a red bulb was lit. The radio shack was an open area across from the chart table, which held the radio gear, a typewriter, and a chair bolted to the deck. The radioman typed the messages that the Communications Officer decoded. Daniel turned around and was handed the message. He read it and then told the Officer of the Day to have the crew go to action stations, but quietly. The word was passed by mouth, and the team diligently stopped what they were doing and got ready for anything. The lights on the ship shifted to red as it was secured.

"Helm come about to this bearing," he said as he passed a note. "This bearing, Aye," he repeated.

He tore up the note and tossed the remains into two different trash cans that had cigarette butts in them. The heat from the embers caused the fresh paper to smolder. Normally he would have passed the note to the scribe who dutifully recorded all orders. This way, where they were going wouldn't be in it. Waisner came to the bridge and informed him that the word had been passed, and the men were ready, willing, and able.

"Good, now have the lookouts alert for downed planes and pilots. We are going to be on this tact for about an hour. Then, we will come to this heading and search some more. A shore party might be required, so have the master at arms pick a dozen men that can be spared and have them meet him at the motor launch as fast as practical."

"Aye, Aye.", he said as he relayed the commands.

The bridge on a PC was the busiest place as it held a radar operations center, a four-by-four closet space that contained a chair and his console. Next to it was the radio shack and the chart room. A ladder in the center of this area led to the sonar workstation; this was at the lowest compartment by the keel, where the hydrophone was placed to optimize acoustics. The space was hardly large enough for more than two crewmen.

One pace behind the bridge was a Yeoman's spartan office with only a typewriter, a small deck, a chair, and a filing cabinet. It was two paces from the chart room, radio, and ladder to below decks and three paces from the wardroom. Here he kept up with the reports that kept the ships running. This was the best place to get the scuttlebutt or gossip about what was happening. It was also easy to see what was being worked on because it was open.

Twenty minutes later, a lookout called, "MAN OVERBOARD!"

He stopped the first mate from hitting the alarm. "Quiet! We are running silent." The man turned red with embarrassment and nodded at the rebuke.

The searchlights were turned on, and they could see a figure floating on the wing of a barely bobbing airplane. He appeared to be unconscious, so they quickly launched the gig, and he told the med bay to be ready to receive casualties. The launch returned fifteen minutes later, and the pilot was winched aboard. He was shaking from the cold; his lips were blue, and the medical crew flew into action with blankets and got him below decks with ruthless efficiency.

"Waisner, you have the bridge. Stay at this heading and let me know if anything comes up."

He sprinted down the corridor to the med bay, the mess hall. It was dead center in the ship. On a PC, the configuration was straightforward. It only consisted of four decks. Two below and one above the main deck. When he arrived, he saw they had stripped the pilot naked and applied warm towels to his skin, massaging him liberally. He awoke, leaned over, and vomited. Luckily, there was a bucket strategically placed there just for that eventuality. His skin and clothing reeked of aviation fuel, and he had undoubtedly swallowed some. The ship's doctor, the Pharmacists Mate, helped him lean up, giving him a swallow of medicinal whiskey. He nodded and whispered, "Thanks." And then leaned over and vomited again.

When he rolled over, his chin was wiped, and he was given a packet of crackers to chew on. He did so, and the color on his face began to change from the grey pallor, and his lips went from blue to barely grey. He saw Daniel and leaned up to give a report. His voice was hoarse, but he managed, "Sir, we went after a six-pack of the enemy and were able to shoot down a Zero and two Oscars. They went into the drink, but the Zero was just there over the horizon at that island. It was coasting in like a glider."

"Good to know. Get some rest. We got you."

He looked to the medical staff and said, "Compartmentalize that," which meant that whatever they had overheard was declared 'secret' or above. They could not discuss it with anyone, even among themselves.

He called to the bridge and asked Waisner to meet him in the Wardroom. When he arrived, he dismissed the staff and closed the door. He double-checked the galley to ensure no one could overhear them, then turned on the radio and tuned it to the Unalaska Station. He pulled out a red codebook, and Waisner understood. A small sideboard was set up with sandwiches and coffee for those hungry between meals. An urn of coffee was next to it, and they helped themselves. Daniel leaned forward when seated and whispered, "The pilot shot down a Zero."

"So what?'

"This one landed over there on that island we are headed for; it might be intact or as close to it as possible. Waisner nodded as he bit into the sandwich. It was tuna salad. He took a swig of coffee and asked, "What are we doing about it?"

"We are going to get there and send a search party. Then, recover it and any intelligence that we can."

"Okay, Skipper. That's what all this cloak and dagger has been about?" Waisner asked.

"Yeah, sorry about that. It was a flash message that just came through."

"Rodger that. I'll see to it. Why don't you get some rest?"

"Sure," Daniel said as he finished up and went to his quarters. He couldn't sleep, so he removed his shirt and shoes and lay there. Finally, he drifted off to sleep, and the next thing he knew, there was a light tapping on his door.

"Come in," he said as he shot upright.

The door opened, and a Yeoman was there, "The XO says to tell you we have arrived."

"I'll be there shortly," he said as he stripped off his t-shirt, used a wet washcloth to freshen up, and donned another one, and a fresh shirt, after which he reached down to put on his shoes.

When he arrived at the bridge, Waisner reported," Sir, we are with the tide, and the shore party is ready to depart, all corked up." They had all donned dark clothing and had used blackened cork on their face to break up their silhouettes.

"Give the word."

"The word is given."

The gig launched with thirteen sailors aboard, shooting out from the ship's port side, a thousand yards from the beach. He watched them disembark with their rifles at the ready. They used flashlights with red lenses to see in the dark without giving their position away. Then, they efficiently made their way up the rocky slope to a bluff. When they arrived, they gave three signal flashes, which meant they had found what they were looking for.

Daniel went over to the radio shack and told the operator, "Send this flash traffic. 'Sushi found. Send the cook.'"

The operator nodded and transmitted. The response was only one word. "Inbound."

After several hours a troop transport ship arrived with heavy equipment and a floating barge. They launched a gig and relieved his men on the bluff. He was ordered to screen the transport, so the shore party were told to report to the wardroom and take the same precautions for secrecy as before. They had turned in their rifles, but all were sporting knives and pistols since they were still at action stations. They were huddled around the table, eating sandwiches and drinking coffee. He informed them that this mission was 'Top Secret' and needed to classify all the information.

All nodded agreement, and they left to turn in their sidearms to the weapons locker when suddenly shots rang out. The ship was hit with tracer fire from the beach on the western side. The Master at Arms pulled his sidearm and returned fire, running to get to the three-inch gun. It was an older kind from 1918 and had barely any cover. He heard a rough grunt or two as men were hit. The Bofors 40mm started to return fire. He grabbed a flare pistol, leaned out to the deck, and fired it. Another one came from the stern. He heard several screams and clashes. He listened to a light chugging and gave the order. "GUNS! GUNS! GUNS! Fire the Rockets!!" The weapons officer, called "GUNS", gave the order and they could barely see a visible shadow. Another Flare was launched into the air. This one did not have a parachute; it was magnesium and exploded, illuminating the target.

The rockets fired two salvos directly at the submarine, striking the bow plane. They could also see a small black rubber raft carrying men to the beach. They lit it up with the 30mm double-barreled autocannons and made short work of it. The sub continued to reverse out of the lagoon that it secreted itself onto.

Waisner was coordinating raising the anchor and getting underway. The only problem was they were screening the transport and could not leave their post.

They heard a sound that resembled a freight train screaming directly into their path. It was the deck gun of the sub firing at them. The transport was also armed, and they returned fire from a higher elevation raking the sub's deck mercilessly until all that remained were ragged hunks of flesh. The sub was wounded and couldn't dive. Then he saw several flashes off to the port side, and the sub exploded.

"TORPEDO in the water. Fifteen thousand yards," called a watchstander. There was nothing that they could do. The Master at Arms swung the 3" gun around and started firing. A sailor came up to the deck with a Lewis gun and started firing wildly over the port side. A Lewis Gun was a machine gun from the Great War with a 97-round drum placed on top and screwed into place. The drum rotated clockwise and fed the ammunition into the chamber. It had a tremendous rate of fire as it launched .303 British or 30.06 Springfield steel jacketed rounds at 500-600 rounds per minute.

The torpedo exploded a few hundred yards away, knocking several of the men down, with a blowback blast shattering the windows. Daniel's cheeks were raked with glass, and he shielded himself with his arms as best he could. He could hear screams and whimpers and was brought back to that fateful day when he was promoted to Warrant.

"SNAP OUT OF IT! Damage reports!" he could hear men rising to their feet and carrying off those injured. Fortunately, the bridge had several redundant men for just such an occasion.

"Reports are coming in, sir. Two wounded and taken to medical. One dead."

"Name of deceased?" he asked as he prepared to write the name in the log.

"Layton Frasier-Scullery."

"Who?"

"The man with the Lewis Gun. His body shielded us from the worst of it."

The TBS Phone rang, and he was informed, "It's the Commodore, sir!" He took the receiver and was told, "Thanks for lighting up that target for us. You are relieved."

"We need to stay at action stations for a while longer. After that, I will need to retire and sound the ship."

"Understood. Carry on" was all that was said.

He hung up and ordered, "Call the Carpenter." Carpenter was meaningless on a modern warship since they were made from steel plates riveted and welded in place. It was a carryover from when they were made of wood. The man was a structural engineer. But the title had stuck.

Waisner had them withdraw to the port side of the transport to check how badly they were damaged. After an hour, they determined some buckling of plating from the explosion, but it presented no loss of structural integrity.

They got underway to return to Dutch Harbor and had a funeral at sea for Layton. All hands were assembled quickly, and what was left of his body had been wrapped in his hammock. They even included a couple of two- by-fours to wrap it correctly and a few chain links to ensure it went to the bottom. Daniel read from the good book, and Layton was laid to rest draped in the American Flag. His body was sent over the side on the board, and the side boys fired a twenty-one-gun salute.

This was not his first-time losing men under his Command. But this was the first time that someone had willingly sacrificed himself. Layton knew what he was doing, but he also knew that if the torpedo struck, they were all doomed. So, he did what he had been trained to do and probably acted without thinking. But his job was in the kitchen, not to be at the bridge or even near it. But sometimes people do what they think is best and Layton had acted, and that action had saved a lot of men.

Daniel pulled out a small black notebook from his breast pocket and wrote the name. He thought back to right before they left Pearl Harbor, he barely had a chance to go over the jackets of each man under his command. He was pretty good at remembering faces and putting names to them was easy. He thought about what to say in the letter that he was going to write. Thinking about what his interactions with Layton had been.

He left his cabin and went down to the scullery where he heard the sounds of his childhood. He had grown up in Charleston, South Carolina, in a large Greek Orthodox family. He was one of thirteen children and even had a twin brother Thanos. He vividly remembered when a neighbor had died, and his mother had taken some Spanakopita over and was shocked at the laughing and carousing that was going on. Their neighbors were an elderly black couple named Ellis and Carmen. Ellis was sitting on the porch with friends and family gathered around, slinging back white lightning, and telling stories of his late wife. He hoisted one up high and yelled, "CARMEN! It won't be long. I'll be joining you soon. The liver is evil and must be punished."

Even though he was only seven at the time, Daniel understood that this wake was a celebration of her life. His mother did not. Snapping back to reality he rounded the corner, and saw the cooks gathered around doing the same thing. He noticed one of them quickly hid a bottle and motioned for it. They all got sullen until he took a swig and handed the hooch back. "Tell me about Layton! I'm sorry that I didn't get to know the man."

"Well, Cap'n. He was from Mount Pleasant."

"Just across the river from where I grew up."

"You don't say?"

"Scout's honor!"

They told him about how Layton's father had worked himself to death trying to provide for his family, and Layton's mother Hetty had taken in laundry and other domestic work as best she could, but there was never enough food. When he was ten, Layton got a hold of some traps, went out to the swamps, and was able to catch various critters. His uncle Boyd had a pushcart that sold cooked meat, and he trundled it up and down the streets selling BBQ, whatever the catch of the day was. Sometimes it was a squirrel, other times possum. Layton was an enterprising youngster and was even hired as a deckhand for fishing boats. He worked for no wages if he could take the residue of the catch home. To him, the food was worth more than the money. He even built a smokehouse and sold smoked meats.

Daniel listened to them tell tales of Layton and all the pranks he pulled. After an hour, he took his leave and returned to his quarters. They had pressed a letter into his hand, telling him to read it before he sent it on to Layton's mother. He was exhausted from all the events of the day and showered, shaved, and got dressed for bed. He opened the letter.

Dear Mom,

If you are reading this, you will have already gotten word that I am dead. Sorry about that. But know this, I am glad to have had the opportunity to serve my country. I want Donna to grow up and be able to accomplish whatever she wants. The world is changing. The Captain is a decent man. He's from back home across the river, and he's square with all of us. The man is absolutely color blind. There is no place for ill-treatment of us here. This is one that I will follow anywhere and lay down my life for him if necessary.

Kiss Donna for me.

Your loving son,

Layton

He folded the letter and then placed it in the slot to be forwarded on. Then he reached for some stationery and began to write.

V-Mail: Hetty Frasier

Mt. Pleasant, SC

July 4, 1942

Mrs. Frasier,

It is with a heavy heart; I regret to inform you of the death of your son Layton. He was a loyal comrade and served with distinction under my Command. He was always willing to pitch in and help with all work required. He completed his tasks with a smile, a nod, or a wink, depending on what was needed. He was fast with a joke and earnest with his fellows. He will be sorely missed. He died protecting over fifteen men on the bridge of my ship. He willingly stepped into the line of fire. Here is a list of men alive today because of your son.

Michael Riley, Jordan Brock, Theodore Lindh, Isaiah Brawley, Levi Schliske, Joseph Schroder, Liebe Barnham, Michael Allen, Elijah Shattuck, David Elliott, Ethan Marcus, Kayden Kloppenburg, Easton Feigl, Jacob Elsner, Brayden Best, Aaron Len, Daniel Core, Matthew Waisner.

I know this seems like a pittance to losing a loved one, but he named you as his life insurance policy beneficiary.

Respectfully Lt. Jg. Daniel Core USN

Commanding Officer PC-234

He climbed into bed and slept without dreaming. He blinked and awoke to them underway. A mess attendant had taken the liberty of bringing him his oatmeal breakfast with cinnamon, raisins, and toast with jam, orange juice, and coffee. It was set up on his small table. He was so tired that he didn't even hear the man come in. He got dressed and finished the meal when the Ensign, Mr. Bettis, arrived. His door was open, and Bettis leaned in and informed him of the condition of the boat and left some reports that needed his signature. He nodded and waved him off.

Next came Waisner, who told him that he was off today and needed rest. He even handed him a note from the Ships Doctor stating the prescription, which was quite amusing since their Ships Doctor was a Pharmacists mate who had no authority. But he played along since the motions had been made. Plus, he could use a day off. The gig was ready to take him to Unalaska whenever he was ready. He chuckled and nodded, "Okay, if you're all going to gang up on me, I'll surrender."

UNALASKA

PC-234 came into the bay and parked in their usual position. The gig dropped Daniel off at the Pier and he walked down to the township. His first stop was "Blackies." He intended to get one of those shots of whiskey. They also had steaks available with all the trimmings. Ordinarily, he could eat in the chow hall, but since there was no Officer's Club, he decided to partake of the local fare.

He had two shots and the steak dinner. He noticed other Officers in there as well. Then, he heard Greek being spoken. He turned around, and there was Thanos Deleganedis. He smiled, rising to his feet, and hugging his friend. They had met while undergoing Combat and Tactics Training in Pearl Harbor. He had just completed officers training, introduced Thanos to southern sweet tea, and informed him about Cheer wine.

"When did you get in?" he asked.

"Late last night."

"What are you running?"

"A PCE." The PCE was a Patrol Craft Escort that was based on a Minesweeper. It was 185 feet long, weighing 640 tons twice his PC's displacement, and had the same 9-foot draft. The total crew complement was 96 men. Because it was larger and sported more weapons, it was slower by two knots. But it had a third more guns available, so it was a good trade off. "How about you?" Thanos asked.

"I've got a PC."

"You notice any problems with the freshwater recycler?"

"Yeah, It doesn't work half the time. That thing hates rough seas."

"I heard about a scuffle last night." Thanos stated.

"Whereabouts?"

"Off to the west."

"Can't say I know anything."

"Really?" Thanos asked, emphasizing the first part of the word.

"Yep. I'm just here enjoying the fifty-cent shots and this steak dinner. Join me?"

"Sure," Thanos said as he sat down.

Daniel motioned to the barkeep, and two shots arrived. "How would you like your steak cooked, sir?"

"Bloody," Thanos said, baring his teeth.

"Coming right up." The man wrote down the order and gave it to the kitchen.

They raised the shots and clinked glasses together. "To absent friends." They tossed them back and slammed the glasses on the table upside down. Not hard enough to break them, but enough to get the point across. Suddenly, they heard other glasses slamming down as all the officers present saw the tribute and followed suit.

They nodded their respects and got back to the visit. "So, what's on the agenda?" Daniel asked.

"Just a mail and supply run. Escorting convoys back and forth." Thanos told him.

"Good. Were you at Midway?" Daniel asked.

"Nope. The Solomons."

"Any news?" Daniel asked

"Not yet. But I have an old newspaper if you want it." Thanos pulled out a copy of the Chicago Sun-Times two weeks out of date.

"Sure. I'll take it."

"I didn't even do the crossword. I think that might be more your thing than mine."

"Chess is more my kind of thing, but heck yeah. I'll do a crossword in a pinch."

The steak arrived, and Thanos dove into it with gusto. The blood was dripping down his chin to his dark cheeks. Thanos was one of those men that always looked like he needed to shave. He had dark hair and thin, pale skin, so he always had what appeared to be a five-o clock shadow. The sight of the undercooked steak made Daniel uncomfortable. He remembered growing up and his mother and father eating raw hunks of meat. He preferred it at least medium. They told him that eating it raw was 'good for the blood!' He could see that Thanos was also a member of that school of thought. He needed to take his mind off the sight of the steak.

"Are you coming on station or just a quick turn around?" Daniel asked.

"Don't know." Thanos said, as he opened an envelope and read his orders, "I've been set up for picket duty for the next three weeks, with escorts to and from Adak."

"What's going on there?"

Thanos scanned the document and said, "Building a Runway."

"Smart. But since the ground is so soggy, how will you get it level enough?" Daniel questioned.

"Oh, that's easy. They have interlocking perforated sheets of steel, called Marston Matting."

"How long is that going to take?"

"Around sixty days, more or less."

"What's the worst thing that you have seen so far?" Daniel asked.

"Well, we had a near miss dockside. This new Ensign came aboard; his only experience had been his college lectures. I was happy that we performed a few drills before we left because he was about to fire a mousetrap before the Chief knocked him down and wrenched the cord from his hand. 'You idiot! You're only supposed to simulate firing.' It would have blown the ship apart and shredded the dock." Thanos finished his meal and reached for his wallet but was waved off.

"You get the next one," Daniel said.

"Okay. Thanks. See you next time."

"Sure thing. Next time."

Thanos rose and departed. Daniel also got up and paid the check, then left. He was looking for anything to do in this desolate place of Quonset huts. He didn't feel like doing much, so he went to the base library and sat down to play a few chess games. He thought back to him showing his daughter Hailey how to play. It was strange because he had only been married to Kim-Yee for a few months before he was shipped out, and both children were from her previous marriage. Hailey was eleven, and Jack only three. But in the short time, he had with them, they had bonded so well that he couldn't imagine life without them. To Jack, he was Poppa. To Hailey, he tried to be just Dad. He was not trying to replace her birth father. He was only picking up the slack. He decided to write to his children.

V-Mail Postcard: Hailey Chung 234 Windward Way
Pearl Harbor, HI, USA

Hey there Hailey,

How are things? Is the summer going well for you? Read any good books lately or played any Chess?

Let me know if you need anything.

Love Dad

P.S. Please give Jack a hug and a kiss from me

He was not very satisfied with the brevity of the message, but it was all he could manage at the time. He dropped the card into the mail slot and returned to the Pier. He informed the Harbor Master of his need to return to his ship and was motored out.

The gig pulled up alongside his Patrol Craft, and he was piped aboard. When he arrived, Waisner pointed to his watch and said, "You're still off duty, Skipper. How about a movie? We've got Cracker Jacks."

"Lead the way."

The time off was good, and he knew he had been hyper-focused on the needs of the men and the ship. The film was "Road to Morocco," the third in a series of films starring Bob Hope and Bing Crosby. It was about two fast-talking men who were castaways that landed in a foreign country and were sold into slavery to a Moroccan Princess. He needed the laughs, and it allowed him to decompress.

After the movie, the cooks set up a buffet of ice cream and cake for the men. He and Waisner stayed and listened to the comrades regale each other over their accomplishments. Blue Section talked about how they had beaten Green sections last time to general quarters." The best time was twenty-five seconds."

"We would have made it if Anderson hadn't tripped and knocked himself silly on the bulkhead."

"Well, there's always next time."

He and Waisner both smiled as the banter went on. After the dessert was finished, he got up, wished his men well, and retired for the evening.

****

The following day he received flash traffic to report to slip twelve and await further instructions. They were going to be part of a protection detail whose job was to lay a submarine net around the mouth of the harbor. It had been assembled on the minelayer, and several frogmen had their gear waiting topside. He instructed his men to be extra vigilant.

After a few days, the task was completed, and he received orders to resume patrol.

USS GRUNION
June 18th, 1942, Aleutian Islands, Alaska

They were out into their patrol sector around Amchika and this night the fog was very dense. The usual sounds were heard over the water when one of the nearby Volcanoes started to belch even more ash and he felt a rumble and saw a black mass headed their way.

Daniel shouted, "ROGUE WAVE! Sound the alarm!" The coxswain barely had time to mash the button before they were swamped.

"HELM TURN INTO THE WAVE! RIDE THE CREST!"

"TURNING INTO THE WAVE AYE!" retorted the helmsman.

"HANG ON!" Daniel yelled as their craft shot up about thirty feet into the air climbing to the top of the wave trying to not get smashed to pieces.

The klaxons were wailing in their typical cries.

They crested the wave and rode it over and down. They slammed into the water again and the shock caused him to bite into his tongue.

"Is everyone all right?"

The bridge crew all groaned in acknowledgement. A few staggered outside to vomit the contents of their stomachs. On the way back to their stations they each grabbed a bottle of seltzer and swished their mouths out and spit into respective trash cans. As they were chugging the contents to try and keep the rest down Daniel asked the question, "Damage reports?"

Waisner said, "Still coming in, Skipper. One or two concussions, a stubbed toe. We're all right so far. Thanks to you."

"Have Mr. Bettis get with the carpenter and sound the ship." "Seriously?"

"Yep. He needs to learn how to do it."

"Aye Aye sir!"

Just then a watch stander called out, "Emergency flare off Starboard!"

"Range?" asked Daniel.

"Five miles!"

"Navigator plot us a course at best speed."

"Is that wise sir? After the hit we just took?"

"It will have to be. We don't have any leaking that we know of, and we don't know how bad they are or even who they are."

"Sparky," Daniel then called to the radioman.

"Sir?"

"Any traffic out there?"

"None sir."

"Navigator call out the plot to helm."

The message was relayed, and they got underway.

An hour or so later they could hear the sound of metal scraping and the noise of the breakers and the sound of men shouting.

"Helm, slow to all stop."

"Slowing to all stop, Aye."

"Drop anchor."

"Anchor dropped," came the reply.

"Launch the gig and have medical on standby."

It took several hours but they were able to ferry the crew off the rocks. All fifty of them.

Once the rescue was complete the Commanding Officer of the Grunion reported to the Bridge. To turn in his records and give the after-action report. "Mr. Cureton, you have the bridge. Captain, come with me." He also motioned for Waisner to follow.

They adjourned to the officer's mess and secured the area against eavesdropping, turning on the radio.

"What happened Captain?" Daniel asked.

"I don't know. We were doing fine and all of a sudden were tossed all over the place and caught by a rip tide. We slammed against the rocks and the hull was ripped open."

"What did you do?"

"We tried our best to keep her afloat, but it was futile. We were out of battery power and couldn't maneuver. So, we got the crew off on a little rubber life raft, only two or three at a time. We were able to retrieve all of the code books and destroyed whatever documents we couldn't take."

"What do you propose to do with the sub?" asked Daniel.

"Scuttle her," the Captain said sadly.

"Are you sure?"

"She's a goner. We've rigged her with explosives all tied to the torpedoes. All you have to do is get to a safe distance and launch a phosphorus shell at the conning tower where we have a box of dynamite. Kinetic energy will take care of the rest."

Waisner finished taking the statement and said, "Sign here, and here."

Daniel stood and strode onto the bridge, "Have gun crew one called forward. Weigh anchor and reverse us to a range of 12,000 yards."

"Rodger that," called Mr. Cureton. "Captain, do you want the bridge back?" he asked in confusion.

"No. You're fine. Once the gun is crewed and ready and we are at a safe distance have them launch one phosphorus shell at the box of dynamite adjacent to the conning tower," Daniel said as he, Waisner, and the submarine captain went out on deck to the forecastle to observe the scuttling.

Several minutes later the tide and engines had carried them to the appropriate distance. He heard the gun crew yell, "Fire in the Hole!" and the gun belched its shell.

They watched it arc lazily towards the boat and then it erupted into a blaze of fireworks. The hull was split in two horizontally and they saw arcs of shrapnel rain up and outwards.

Mr. Cureton gave the orders, and they headed back to Dutch Harbor for debrief.

Once there he received further orders to return to Pearl for rest, refit, and replenishment. He was given leave for a week while the plates were hammered out at the Yards. So, they steamed away and headed for home. While they were underway, all men trained to become a jack of all trades in operating, maintaining, and fighting the ship. If any man got injured or killed, they could all fill the billet. They even had some enlisted men serve as junior officers of the day to give others a rest. Since the crew compliment was so low, the largest segment of ratings on board was in the engineering section. Typically, four men served watches underway in the engine room; one served as a fireman and two as throttle men, with the last being a messenger, gauge reader, or handyman. The men were all close-knit and recognized each other's strengths and weaknesses. They even had a ship's cat named Mimi, who had delivered kittens in the crossing.

When they arrived, their families were waiting on the docks, cheering them on. He turned command of the ship over to Ensign Bettis and told him he would be sure to return the favor when they were in a port of his choosing. Bettis nodded agreement and wished him well. Shaking his hand, Bettis secretly placed an item in his coat pocket.

HOMECOMING
August 15, 1942

He and Waisner disembarked as well as twenty crewmen. Since the complement was 65, a third was all they should manage at any time. He went through the security gate into his wife's loving arms. Kim-Yee was a petite Chinese woman with long black hair who had lovely almond-shaped eyes. You couldn't tell by looking at her that she was nearing forty. Her Nurse's crisp white Navy uniform fit her smartly, and she was wearing a red sweater over it. She had very long legs and a short trunk which was unusual on her 5'1' frame. He once heard a sailor's remark aboard a ship about a woman "who had legs that went up to her neck." Now he understood the reference.

Hailey, her mother's spitting image, gave him a big hug and was nearly as tall as her mother. She was almost twelve, and he reminded himself to celebrate her birthday before he shipped out. He needed to spend some quality time with her. So, he decided to take her to breakfast the first chance he got to catch up.

Miranda was Kim-Yee's sister and an older version of her. She always dressed a little severely, and today she wore a grey business- type suit. She was holding Jack, a rambunctious four-year-old squirming to get to his 'Poppa.' She finally relented, and he took off like a shot, weaving his way through the crowd expertly to run into Daniel's arms. Daniel had stooped down low and grabbed him, then rose high and held him aloft, with Jack squealing in delight. Then kisses all around. They walked to the Wagoneer that they referred to as 'The Beast!'. Miranda got into the driver's seat and carefully ensured no one was around before she pulled out. He could tell she had experience with the car and was extra nervous since so many people were milling around excitedly talking.

They drove the twenty minutes to their base housing, a quaint yellow bungalow across from the beach. It had such good airflow that they sometimes opened all the windows and let the breezes come through. It was nature's air conditioning.

As they walked up the steps on the porch, he could smell the telltale aroma of Chinese cooking. His mouth watered, and he asked Miranda playfully, "Hey, Sis, what's cooking?"

"What do you think?" she asked in the same tone.

"Let's see. White rice, oyster mushrooms, mashed potatoes, gravy, and ham?

She smiled and opened the door to reveal a delectable spread on the table. Miranda and Kim-Yee donned aprons, went to the cast iron stove, and began placing mittens on their hands to put the warm food on the table.

Hailey and Jack went to the bathroom to wash up, and he noticed that both had grown in the two months he had been away. Jack by an inch, and Hailey was sporting slight muscle definition on her arms. Both children also had deep dark tans from going to the beach. He noticed she was scrubbing her face furiously and smirked as to why. Puberty.

The food was placed, and they all sat down. Jack was no longer in his highchair and had a booster seat. He had recently turned four in May, and his mother had decided he was getting too big for some things. Hailey's face was also changing slightly, he noticed her cheekbones were more pronounced, but she was still squinting. So, he reminded himself to ask his wife about that when he got a chance.

Chopsticks flew across the table as they grabbed what they wanted or needed from the spread. Asian table manners differed from Americans. The rice was served first, with every person getting a bowl. Then, the lids were removed from the dishes, and each person used a spoon or chopsticks to get their portion. He saw that Jack had a smaller pair of lacquered black chopsticks by his place setting but didn't use them. He preferred the silver spoon that he had grown up eating from.

Sweet tea was on the table, and he switched his chopsticks to his right hand and used his left to pick up the glass and take a swallow.

He replied, "Ah. That's good," then he resumed eating. They all just smiled. He was no stranger to chopsticks as he had been stationed in the Orient for roughly two years in what seemed another life. He had joined in 1939 when he witnessed German U-boats sinking ships from a convoy headed to Britain that had launched from Charleston, SC. He even had a Captains ticket, as his grandfather had been a tugboat captain and wanted to leave the business to a member of the family, and he seemed to be the only one interested. So, he had worked tirelessly for a year to earn that Captain's Certificate, and then the world went crazy. After witnessing the destruction of the ships, he went home, and when he walked in, his grandfather just knew. He didn't have to say anything. Grandad just got up and began packing a seabag handing it to him.

"If a good man does nothing, then that is evil enough. Go forth and help conquer that evil. But remember, you will only be a wheel in a cog. They will tell you your place. Please don't fight with them or argue because cream rises, no matter what. Your time will come."

They had got in the truck, and he went to the induction site. He disembarked, never looking back.

The Navy had sent him to basic, then on to gunnery school. He made it to the rate of second class and was pretty good at what he did but always struggled with math. They wouldn't even consider him for a Warrant Officer, which he felt was unfair, but then he remembered his grandfather's wisdom and just shrugged it off. Then his ship was attacked in the Coral Sea, and all the officers were killed. Before he died, Mr. Begley pinned the rank of Warrant Officer to his collar. He had acting Captaincy and was told to "FIGHT THE SHIP." The Captain had left a battlefield promotion in his safe for this eventuality. Daniel fought off the enemy, the elements, the fires, and the sea. He got the ship and crew to safety and was escorted to the Commodore, who took his statement and sent him off to Pearl Harbor to see Admiral Nimitz, who was impressed and set him up at Officers Candidacy School.

While waiting for his slot to open, he met Kim-Yee, and the two had a whirlwind romance. He graduated and was commissioned as a Lieutenant Junior Grade. This allowed him to skip the rank of Ensign. Kim-Yee had been at the ceremony in San Francisco and had even hitched a ride with Nimitz to be there. She had dropped the bombshell of their age difference and that she had two children from a previous marriage. He didn't care. He proposed to her, and they married immediately. Now, looking back, he couldn't imagine a life without them.

He was snapped out of his reverie by Kim-Yee fussing at Hailey over a second helping of rice. Even though he could barely understand his wife's language, she was cross with her and kept shoving vegetables into her bowl. Hailey was almost in tears, and then Kim-Yee said something harsh, and her face turned white. Hailey whirled out of her chair and ran to the veranda. At the same time, Kim-Yee stormed to the back door. He was torn, but he knew his wife's temper, and she needed time to cool off. So, he decided to go to Hailey to see what the matter was. He could hear her crying loudly and just walked up behind her. She whirled and buried herself into him in a hug. The sobs were so strong that she was shaking. "I'm sorry to ruin your homecoming, dad!"

"There, there, sweetie. What's going on?"

"Mom didn't want me to have more rice."

"I could see that. But there is something else happening here."

"She said I needed to eat more vegetables to stay skinny and attract a husband. But I'm so hungry all the time."

He motioned for her to be seated and said, "You are hungry all the time because your body is being flooded with hormones as you enter puberty."

"Is that why my face is constantly oily.?"

"Yes."

"What's this puberty like?"

"Well, it's different for everyone. Boys and girls alike. For example, my twin brother and I had the opposite experience with it. He bulked up around twelve, had facial hair, and gained thirty-five pounds of muscle. On the other hand, I looked like I was twelve until my eighteenth summer. I couldn't even shave until recently. I had three little chest hairs, and that was all. I was a runt."

She giggled at that. "But you turned out fine after all."

"Yes, but it's a biological process. Your body changes day by day or not at all. You could grow in spurts or by leaps and bounds. It's a complete unknown."

"My clothes don't fit me right anymore."

"So, let's go out and get you some new ones. School starts in a couple of weeks."

"Okay."

"Now get back to the table, and I'll sort out your mom."

He calmly walked to the back of the house where Kim-Yee was sitting on the stoop with her head hung low. "Want to talk about it?"

She sighed. "I'm a terrible mother."

"What makes you say that?"

"I said something unforgivable."

"And what was that?"

"I called her Ton Fa."

"Rice Bucket."

"Yes, but it's also a cruel insult. It's saying she is a fatty."

"How so?"

"It implies that she is overeating rice."

"But she is a growing young woman."

"She's just a girl."

"Not anymore. That biological clock just went tick-tock."

"What do you mean?"

"She is always scrubbing her face because it's oily."

"It's only because she eats too many snacks and not the good ones. She's eating potato chips and sugar sandwiches."

"Sugar sandwiches?"

"Yes, those fried pies and sweets in wax paper."

"Like Moon Pies?"

"Yes. Then she chases it down with sodas. Too much sugar. That's what makes her fat."

"She's not fat. She is large-boned. Wait until you meet my sister Lyra; your entire attitude will change. But she's almost twelve. Why would you push her about being skinny for a husband? If a suitor doesn't like her as is, he can hit the bricks."

"What?"

"Keep moving."

"Oh."

"What else is bothering you?"

"Tan-Fa is what Garry and his whole family used to call me. He said that I should be grateful that he had rescued me from a life of poverty. I don't have a typical Chinese body. I'm not slender like the other girls."

"No. You have nice curves. You were raised in a colony with excellent medical care and better access to food and nutrition than most others. This caused you to be larger. But their yardstick for healthy is vastly different. If you don't get enough nutrition early in life, it can stunt your growth. They also probably had limited access to food and rationed everything. Hence why they considered a second helping of rice a faux pas. Now Hailey is facing the same thing. Her access to medical care and nutrition is superior to yours so that she will be bigger than you. She also will not have a typical Chinese body either. But I saw that she was still squinting. I thought you took her and Miranda to see the eye doctor?"

"I did, and they both received two pairs of glasses."

"I see. Well, I'll follow up with Hailey on that one later. By the way, after dinner, I'm going to take her shopping for clothes. Just have some quality father-daughter time."

"Okay."

"Let's get back to the table before the food gets cold."

They returned to the table and ate in relative silence. He helped clear the dishes, and that was when he noticed that his coat pocket was moving. When he came in, he had draped it across the chair in the living room without thinking. He heard a slight mewling and opened the pocket to find a tiny black kitten. Jack came over, and held his hand out excitedly, Daniel gently passed him the kitten. Miranda heard the meowing and went out of the kitchen with a small saucer of milk and motioned for Jack to place it on the floor. He did, and the kitten could barely stand but found the milk and was greedily lapping it up. "What do we call it?"

"Her," said Miranda as she studied the anatomy of the kitten.

"Mimi?" Daniel asked.

"Mimi!", said Jack agreeing to the name.

Hailey and Kim-Yee came into the kitchen to see what was happening and were mesmerized.

"Where did she come from?" Kim-Yee asked excited.

"The ship. Our cat had delivered a litter, and Mr. Bettis must have snuck her into my coat when I departed."

"Why would he do that?"

"Because we only have room for maybe two cats."

"Why have any aboard?" asked Hailey.

"To keep the mice and rats at bay."

"Why would rodents be on board at all?" asked Kim-Yee.

"Because wherever there is food, there are vermin."

"Are we keeping her?" asked Hailey as she gushed over the kitten.

"Sure. But we need to have some soft food available."

Miranda said, "Steamed fish and rice together will be fine."

"Okay. That's settled. Right Mimi?" he asked as he stroked her silken coat.

"She's quite a little purr factory, isn't she?" remarked Kim-Yee as she picked her up and searched for a shoebox to put her in. She used one of Daniels's old t-shirts and a wind-up clock placed underneath. That would mimic the mother's heartbeat, and she would fall asleep quickly. True to form, she did within five minutes.

He stretched and told them he would take Hailey out to buy clothing. He then went to take a shower and change into his civilian clothes, got the keys to the sports car, and they went shopping.

They drove to Sears on South Beretania Street just east of Kalakaua Ave. It had opened last December and had the latest styles. It was an upgrade from the catalog store that they had before. He parked the car, and they went in. The saleswoman snapped her up and quickly asked Daniel, "Will she be needing one of everything?"

"Yes, ma'am. I think she will even need a training bra," he said sheepishly.

She was brisk and efficient. "No problem. Come back in an hour, and we will have her all sorted out."

"One thing. She hates dresses, but she will need at least two. One black and one for church."

"Noted. Now run along, sir. She is in good hands."

Since he had some time to kill, he went to the hardware department and selected a toolkit for general use around the house. He returned an hour later, and they were boxing up the last of her clothing. He was presented with the bill, and they asked him about opening a charge account. He declined and wrote a check. He could have signed a slip and had it drafted against his pay, but that wasn't like him. He and his wife preferred to pay for things that they needed immediately. They were just practical people who had been raised that way. They put the purchases in the trunk and walked around the area, enjoying the day. He spotted a hot dog cart, and they selected a chili dog each and two coca colas. He also got two bags of chips, and they sat on a bench nearby. She dove into hers with gusto and slugged the soda quickly.

"Whoa, their sport. Don't eat so fast that you bite the inside of your cheek."

"Sorry, dad. But I'm hungry right now."

"I get it, and it's a real treat. Your mom would go apoplectic if she saw us eating this. I won't tell if you won't," he said conspiratorially.

"I'll make sure not to get any chili on me," she said as she polished it off.

"I'm sorry that I'm gone so much."

"Don't apologize, Dad. I know. We are at war; at least we have enough to eat and don't have to worry about being attacked here, and you can come back from time to time."

"That's just it. We already have been, and I'm trying to keep that from happening again. But we have been invaded."

Her face drained of all color, "What? Where?"

"An outer island off the coast of Alaska. I shouldn't be telling you this, but I want you to know that my absence is important. No! Vital to the safety and security of everyone. I am missing pieces of your childhood and am trying to end this war. But you can't repeat what I told you unless it appears in the newspaper, radio, or newsreel. Deal?"

"Deal," she agreed.

They noticed a government car pull into a space next to them, and a military driver got out and opened the door. Nimitz called out, "Hop in!"

"Sir, I'm with my daughter."

"She can come along, too."

They looked at each other and shrugged, then complied.

After they were seated, Nimitz made nice to Hailey, "I'm sorry to have to steal him away like this, but..."

"It's important. I get it, sir," she said, trying to put on a brave face. They dropped her off at the house several minutes later and then raced off to Nimitz's office. Once she was out of the car, the briefing began.

"So, that plane you helped acquire was a treasure trove of info." It's the closest to intact that we have, and the pilot even had a codebook on him. We were fortunate that he crash-landed on land because the ink on them is designed to bleed out quickly when exposed to water. Did you know that they have a heating unit in the cockpit plugged directly into their flight suits? And they have an underwear layer that is made of silk?"

"No, sir, I didn't"

"Remarkable times that we are living in."

"Yes, sir."

"We were able to fabricate the parts necessary to get that plane flying again and ran it through twenty-five test flights, where we discovered it has two Achilles heels. It has a lousy carburetor; while diving, it sputters and loses speed and efficiency. Therefore, it could be an easy target for your gunners. Two, it can't perform rolls at moderately high rates of speed."

"Sir?"

"Yes?"

"Why am I here?"

"Oh, yes. Sorry about that. Your medals came in, and the ones for your men; we wanted to hold a ceremony."

"There's more to this than that, or you wouldn't be dancing around the issue."

"You got me. There will be PR men there who want your story. I've been fending them off and keeping you on classified missions as long as possible to delay the inevitable, but it's finally here."

"Why me?"

"Because people need a hero, and you came from other ranks. We must sell War Bonds if we are to have the money necessary to win this war."

"I'm not very good with meeting and greeting and kissing babies.

That's the work of politicians, actors, and dignitaries."

"Well, pucker up, buttercup! We will get you some knee pads, lip balm and lessons, but you will give them what they want, and you will like doing it."

"Yes, sir," he said defeatedly.

"One thing."

"What is it?"

"Leave my family out of it. I've seen this type of thing get ugly."

"No, worries. We won't even tell them that you are married if

that helps. But that can come with its dangers. Women throwing themselves at you, etc. On Tuesday, you will report to Hanger 12 for the ceremony at 10:00 in Full Dress Uniform."

"Rodger, sir!" he said as he saluted and left the building. He was driven back to his car and then went home. He parked the vehicle, took his shoes off, entered the house, brought the packages inside, and placed them on the sofa. He asked Miranda where the children were.

"Outside weeding and watering the Victory Garden," she said proudly.

"Where's Kim-Yee?"

"Sis is taking a nap."

"Right. Thanks." He headed to the bedroom, where he found his wife snoring with a wet washcloth over her eyes. He took off his shirt and laid down next to her. She instinctively rolled over and kissed him while fully asleep. He held her in his arms until Hailey came to wake him for dinner.

They both got up and went to the kitchen, where the leftovers from lunch were on display. He tucked in, and they ate in relative silence.

After dinner, once the dishes were washed, they all settled into the living room and gathered around the radio to listen to one of the President's Fireside Chats.

"My fellow Americans:

It has been months since we were attacked at Pearl Harbor. For the two before that attack, this country had been gearing itself up to a high level of production of munitions. And yet our war efforts had done little to dislocate the normal every day of most of us.

Since then, we have dispatched strong forces of our Army and Navy, several hundred thousand of them, to bases and battlefronts thousands of miles from home. We have stepped up our war production on a scale that tests industrial power, (and) our engineering genius, and our economic structure to the utmost. We have had no illusions about the fact that this is a tough job—and a long one.

American warships are now in combat in the North and South Atlantic, in the Arctic, in the Mediterranean, in the Indian Ocean, and the North and South Pacific. American troops have taken stations in South America, Greenland, Iceland, the British Isles, the Near East, the Middle East and the Far East, the Continent of Australia, and many islands of the Pacific. American warplanes, manned by Americans, are flying in actual combat over all the continents and oceans.

On the front, the most crucial moment was, without question, the crushing counter-offensive on the part of the great armies of Russia against the powerful German army. These Russian forces have destroyed and are destroying more armed power of our enemies—troops, planes, tanks, and guns—than all the other United Nations put together.

In the Mediterranean area, matters remain on the surface much as they were. But the situation there is receiving very meticulous care.

Recently, we (have) received news of a change in government in what we used to know as the Republic of France- a name dear to the hearts of all lovers of liberty—a name and an institution that we hope will soon be restored to full dignity.

Throughout the Nazi occupation of France, we have hoped for the maintenance of a French Government which would strive to regain independence, reestablish the principles of "Liberty, Equality, and Fraternity, " and restore France's historical culture that has been consistent from the very beginning. However, we are now greatly concerned lest those who have recently come to power may seek to force the brave French people into submission to Nazi despotism.

The United Nations will take measures, if necessary, to prevent the use of French territory in any part of the world for military purposes by the Axis powers. The good people of France will readily understand that such action is essential for the United Nations to prevent assistance to the armies or navies or air forces of Germany, Italy (and) or Japan. The overwhelming majority of the French people understand that the fight of the United Nations is fundamentally their fight, that our victory means the restoration of a free and independent France—and the saving of France from the slavery which would be imposed upon her by her external enemies and by her internal traitors.

We know how the French people really feel. We have a deep-seated determination to obstruct every step in the Axis plan extending from occupied France through Vichy France to all the people in every ocean and continent.

Our planes are helping in the defenses today; in defense of Flying Fortresses will be fighting for the liberation of the darkened continent of Europe itself.

In all the occupied countries, there are men and women, and even little children who have never stopped fighting, never stopped resisting, never stopped proving to the Nazis that their so-called "New Order" will never be enforced upon free peoples.

In the German and Italian peoples, themselves, there is a growing conviction that the cause of Nazi-ism and Fascism is hopeless—that their political and military leaders have led them along the bitter road which leads not to world conquest but final defeat. They cannot fail to contrast the present frantic speeches of these leaders with their arrogant boastings of a year ago and two years ago.

And on the other side of the world, we have passed through a phase of severe losses in several places in the Far East.

We have inevitably lost control of a large portion of the Philippine Islands. But this whole nation pays tribute to the Filipino and American officers and men who held out so long on the Bataan Peninsula, to those fierce and gallant fighters who still hold Corregidor, where the flag flies, and to the forces (which) that are still striking effectively at the enemy on Mindanao and other islands.

The Malayan Peninsula and Singapore are in the hands of the enemy Netherlands; East Indies are almost entirely occupied, though resistance continues. Many other islands are in possession of the Japanese. But there is good reason to believe that the southward advance has been checked. Australia, New Zealand, and many other territories will be bases for offensive measures, and we are, determined that the territory (which) that has been lost will be regained.

The Japanese are pressing their northward advance against Burma with considerable power, driving toward India and China. They were opposed with great bravery by small British and Chinese forces aided by American fliers.

The news in Burma tonight is not good. The Japanese may cut the Burma Road, but I want to say to the gallant people of China that no matter what advances the Japanese may make, ways will be found to deliver airplanes and munitions of war to the armies of Generalissimo Chiang Kai-shek.

We remember that the Chinese people were the first to stand up and fight against the aggressors in this war, and in the future (an) a still unconquerable China will play its proper role in maintaining peace and prosperity, not only in Eastern Asia but in the whole world.

For every advance the Japanese have made since starting their frenzied career of conquest, they have had to pay a heavy toll on warships, transports, planes, and in. They are feeling the effects of those losses. Japan even reported that our air force had dropped bombs on Tokyo and other centers of Japanese war industries. If this is true, it is the first time in history that Japan has suffered such indignities.

Although the treacherous attack on Pearl Harbor was the immediate cause of our entry into the war, that event found the American people spiritually prepared for war on a worldwide scale went into this war fighting. We know what we are fighting for. We realize that the war has become what Hitler originally claimed it to be—a total war.

Not all of us can have the privilege of fighting our enemies in distant parts of the world."

Daniel looked at his wife and held her hand. She squeezed back fiercely knowing that they had both been thrown into the maelstrom on that fateful day.

The president's speech went on," Not all of us can have the privilege of working in a munitions factory or a shipyard, or on the farms or in oil fields or mines, producing the weapons or the raw materials that are needed by our armed forces.

But there is one front and one battle where everyone in the United States

—every man, woman, and child—is in action be privileged to remain in action throughout this war. That front is right here at home, in our daily lives, (and) in our daily tasks. Here at home, everyone has the privilege of whatever self-denial is necessary, not only to supply our fighting men but to keep the economic structure of our country fortified and secure during and after the war.

This will require, the abandonment not only of luxuries but of many other creature comforts.

Every loyal American is aware of his individuality. Whenever I hear anyone saying "The American people are complacent—they need to be aroused," I feel like asking him to come to Washington (and) to read the mail that floods into the White House and all departments of this Government. The one question that recurs through thousands of letters and messages is, "What more can I do to help my country win this war"? To factories, (and) win materials, (and) to pay the labor, (and) to provide transportation, (and) equip and feed and house the soldiers, sailors, and marines (and) to do all the thousands of things necessary in a war—all cost a lot of money, more money than has ever been spent by any nation at any time in the long history of the world.

We are now spending, solely for war purposes, the sum of about one hundred million dollars every day until this year is over, that almost unbelievable rate of expenditure will be doubled.

All of this money has to be spent—and spent quickly if we are to produce within the time now available the enormous quantities of weapons of war pending these tremendous sums present the grave danger of disaster to our national economy.

When your Government continues to spend these unprecedented sums for munitions month by month and year by year, that money goes into the pocketbooks and bank accounts of the people of the United States. At the same time, raw materials and many manufactured goods are necessarily taken away from civilian use, and taken away from civilian use, and machinery and factories. If a professor of mathematics or economics sees that if people with plenty of cash start bidding against each other for scarce goods, the price of those goods (them) goes up.

Yesterday I submitted to the Congress of the United States a seven-point program, a program of general principles which, taken together, could be called the national economic policy for attaining the great objective of keeping the cost of living down. I repeat them now to you in substance: First, through taxes, we must not forget to provide opportunities and corporate profits at a low, we must have; reasonable low wages. "

Jack piped up," Daddy do we have to listen to this?"

"Yes son. We do. It's important."

"It's boring."

"Then read your comic book.", Daniel said as he turned his attention back to the speech.

"Fourth, we must stabilize farm prices.

Fifth, we must put more billions into War Bonds.

Sixth, we must ration all scarce essential commodities.

Seventh, we must discourage installment buying and encourage paying off debts and mortgages.

I do not think it is necessary to repeat what I said yesterday to Congress in discussing these general principles. The important thing to remember and it's critical that everyone is that every one of these points depends on this program to work.

Some people are already taking the position that every one of the seven points is missing the point, which sites, on their own, individuals seem very willing to approve of self-denial—on the part of their neighbors. The only effective course of action is a simultaneous attack on all factors that increase the cost of living, in one comprehensive, all-embracing program covering prices, profits, wages, taxes, and debts.

The blunt fact is that every person in the United States will receive this program. Some of you will be affected more directly by one or two of these restrictive measures, but all of you will be affected indirectly. Businessmen's man, or do you own stock in a business corporation? Well, your profits are going to, a reasonably low level by taxation. Your income will be subject to higher taxes. Indeed, in these times, when every available dollar should go to the war effort, I do not think that any American citizen should have a net income in excess of over per year after payment of taxes.

Are you a retailer or a wholesaler or a manufacturer or a farmer, or a landlord? Ceilings are being placed on the prices at which you can sell your goods or rent your property.

Do you work for wages? You will have to forego higher wages for your particular job for the duration of the war.

All of us are used to spending money for things want, things, however, which are not absolutely essential. We will forego that kind of spending. Best put every dime and every dollar, we can spare out of our earnings into War Bonds and Stamps. Because the demands of the war effort required the rationing of goods needed, the war demands. Because the stopping of purchases of non-essentials will release thousands of workers who are needed in the war effort.

As I told Congress yesterday, "sacrifice" is not exactly the proper word with which to describe this program of self-denial. At the end of this great struggle, we shall have saved our freeway and shall have made no " sacrifice."

The price for civilization must be paid in hard work, sorrow, and blood. The price is not too high. If you doubt it, ask those millions who live today under the tyranny of Hitlerism.

Ask the workers of France and Norway, and the Netherlands, whipped to labor by the lash, whether the stabilization of wages is too great a "sacrifice."

Ask the farmers of Poland and Denmark, of Czechoslovakia and France, who looted of their livestock, starving while their own crops were stolen from their land, and ask whether "parity" prices are too great a "sacrifice." Ask the businessmen of Europe, whose enterprises have been stolen from their owners, whether the limitation of profits and personal incomes is too great a "sacrifice."

Ask the women and children whom Hitler is starving whether the rationing of tires and gasoline and sugar is too great a " sacrifice."

We do not have to ask them. They have already given us their agonized answers.

This great war effort must be carried through to its victorious conclusion by the indomitable will and determination of the people as one great whole.

It must not be impeded by the faint of heart.

It must not be impeded by those who put their own selfish interests above the interests of the nation's interests be impeded by those who pervert honest criticism into a statement of fact.

It must not be impeded by self-styled experts either in economics or military problems who know neither accurate figures nor geography itself. It must not be impeded by a few bogus patriots who use the sacred freedom of the press to echo the sentiments of the propagandists in Tokyo and Berlin.

And, above all, it shall not be imperiled by the handful of noisy traitors—betrayers of America, (and) betrayers of Christianity itself—would-be dictators who in their hearts and souls have yielded to Hitlerism and would have this Republic do likewise.

I shall use all of the executive power that I have to carry out the policy laid down. If it becomes necessary to ask for any additional legislation in order to attain our objectivating a spiral in the cost of living, I shall do so. I know the American farmer, the American workman, and the American businessman. I know that they will gladly embrace this economy and equality of sacrifice, satisfied that it is necessary for the most vital and compelling motive in all their lives—winning through to victory.

Never in the memory of man has there been a war in which the courage, the endurance, and the loyalties of civilians played so vital a part.

Many thousands of civilians worldwide have been and are worldwide aimed by enemy action. Indeed, it was the grit of the common people of Britain under fire Britain common people under fire are from winning the war in 1940. The ruins of London and Coventry and other cities are today the proudest monuments to British heroism.

Our own American civilian population is now relatively safe from such disasters. And, to an ever-increasing extent, our soldiers, sailors, and marines are fighting with great bravery and great skill on far distant fronts to make sure that we shall remain safe.

Miranda was doing her knitting and remarked," Aya. It's so sad!"

The radio droned on, "I should like to tell you one or two stories about the men we have in our armed forces:

There is, for (instance) example, Dr. Corydon M. Wassell. He was a missionary, well known for his good works in China. He was a simple, modest, retiring man, nearly sixty years old, but he entered the service of his country and was commissioned a Lieutenant Commander in the Navy.

Dr. Wassell was assigned to duty in Java, caring for wounded officers and men of the cruisers HOUSTON and MARBLEHEAD, which had been in heavy action in the Java seas.

When the Japanese advanced across the island, it was decided to evacuate as many as possible of the wounded to Australia. But about twelve of the men were so badly wounded that they couldn't (not) be moved. Dr.

Wassell remained with (these men), knowing that he would be captured by the enemy. But he decided to make a last desperate attempt to get the men out of Java. He asked each of them if he wished to take the chance, and everyone agreed.

He first had to get the twelve men to the seacoast—fifty miles away. To do this, he had to improvise stretchers for the hazardous journey. The men were suffering severely, but Dr. Wassell kept them alive by skill and inspired them with his own courage.

And as the official report said, Dr. Wassell was "almost like a Christ-like shepherd devoted to his flock."

On the seacoast, he embarked the men on a little Dutch ship. They were bombed, (and) they were machine-gunned by waves of Japanese planes. Dr. Wassell took virtual command of the ship and, by extraordinary skill, avoided destruction, hiding in (small) little bays and little inlets.

A few days later, Dr. Wassell and his (little) small flock of wounded men reached Australia safely.

And today, Dr. Wassell (now) wears the Navy Cross.

Another story concerns a ship, a ship rather than an individual man. You may remember the tragic sinking of the submarine, the U.S.S. SQUALUS off the New England coast in the summer of 1939. Some of the crew were lost, but others were saved by the speed and efficiency of the surface rescue crews. The SQUALUS itself was tediously raised from the bottom of the (ocean) sea.

She was repaired and put back into commission, and eventually, she sailed again under a new name, the U.S.S. SAILFISH. Today, she is a potent and effective unit of our submarine fleet in the Southwest Pacific. The SAILFISH has covered many thousands of miles in operations in (the) those (western Pacific) waters.

She has sunk a Japanese destroyer.

She has torpedoed a Japanese cruiser.

She has made (two) torpedo hits—two of them—on a Japanese aircraft carrier.

Three of the enlisted men of our Navy who went down with the SQUALUS in 1939 and were rescued are today serving on the same ship, the U.S.S. SAILFISH, in this war.

It seems to me that it is heartening to know that the SQUALUS, once given up as lost, rose from the depths to fight for our country in times of peril.

One more story (which) that I heard only this morning:

This is a story of one of our Army Flying Fortresses operating in the Western Pacific. The pilot of this plane is a modest young man, proud of his crew for one of the most brutal fights a bomber has yet experienced. The bomber departed from its base, apart or a flight of five bombers, to attack Japanese transports (which) that were landing troops against us in the Philippines. When they had gone about halfway to their destination, one of the motors of this bomber went out of commission. The young pilot lost contact with the other bombers. The crew, however, got the motor working, got it going again, and the plane proceeded on its mission alone.

By the time it arrived at its target, the other four Flying Fortresses had already passed over, had dropped their bombs, and had stirred up the hornets' nest of Japanese " Zero" planes. Eighteen of (them) these " Zero" fighters attacked our one Flying Fortress. Despite this mass attack, the aircraft proceeded on its mission and dropped all of its bombs on six Japanese transports lined up along the docks, returning on its homeward journey, a running fight between the bomber and the eighteen Japanese pursuit planes continued for seventy-five miles. Four pursuit (ships) planes of the Japs attacked simultaneously at each side. (and) Four were shot down with the side guns. During this fight, the bomber's radio operator was killed, the engineer's right hand was shot off, and one gunner was crippled, leaving only one man available to operate both side guns. Although wounded in one hand, the gunner alternately manned both side guns, bringing down three more Japanese "Zero" planes. While this was going on, one engine on the American bomber was shot out, one gas tank was hit, the radio was shot off, and the oxygen system was completely destroyed. Out of eleven control cables, all but four were shot away. The rear landing wheel was blown off completely, and the two front wheels were both destroyed.

The fight continued until the remaining Japanese pursuit ships exhausted their ammunition and turned back. With two engines gone and the plane practically out of control, the American bomber returned to its base after dark and made an emergency landing. The mission had been accomplished.

The name of that pilot is Captain Hewitt T. Wheless of the United States Army. He comes from a place in Texas—with a population of 2,375. He has been awarded the Distinguished Service Cross. And I hope that he is listening.

These stories I have told you are not exceptional. They are typical examples of individual heroism and skill.

As we here at home contemplate our own duties, our duties and responsibilities, let us think and think hard about the example of these fighting men.

Our soldiers and sailors are members of well-disciplined units. But they are still and forever individuals—free individuals. They are farmers, workers, businessmen, professional men, artists, and clerks. They are the United States of America.

That is why they fight.

We, too, are the United States of America.

That is why we must work and sacrifice.

It is for them. It is for us. It is for victory."

Kim-Yee got up and turned the radio off, knowing it would play on every station. She grabbed a big band record and put it on the turntable, and she and Hailey danced to Moonlight Sonata.

Meanwhile, Jack was playing checkers but using chess pieces, and Miranda was knitting something. Daniel just drank his beer and took it all in. He was enjoying what little family life he had.

He thought about his brothers who were out there somewhere fighting to ensure that what happened in Europe stayed over there. He got up and went to his office grabbing the valise and pulling out the letters that he had received.

One was from his little sister Diana; it was an actual letter that had been secreted in a box of baked goods. He noticed her spidery handwriting and saw the excellent attention to detail as she meticulously spelled every word taking great care to inform them of their sister Thea flying planes for the civil air patrol.

Dear Brothers,

I know that everyone is doing their part for the war effort and now the wild child is at it again. She was seeing that boy Lee Skipper who has always been a bit rowdy Well, his uncle Dave has a crop-dusting plane and Lee took T up in it one night and she was hooked. Lee has always treated her well and didn't mind when I tagged along with her a time or two. Anyway, she joined up with the coastal watchers and when an opening came up for the Civil Air Patrol she immediately went down and signed up. Now she goes out most days screaming around the skies. I don't think she ever wants to land that thing.

In other news, there are a lot of soldiers, sailors, and airmen in the area for coastal defense. This means that the USO throws a lot of dances and parties. Momma makes us go to them, but I don't like it. Being pawed at by officers. I prefer to go see the real men and dance with them as they are in the thick of it and they are always respectful and grateful whereas the officers treat us as objects. The curfews and blackout are depressing but we are at war, and it can't be helped. Know that I pray for each and every one of you, every day. I want you all to return home safe and sound. I know that might not be possible, but I can sleep safely knowing that you all are out there doing your duty.

Your loving sister,

Diana

On Tuesday morning, Daniel donned his dress uniform, and they all got on their Sunday best and drove to the Hangar for the Ceremony. The awards were pinned, and he saw Restivo again who was the sole surviving member of the bridge crew on his first ship, the Destroyer USS Aberdeen. There were photographers from Stars and Stripes, and they crowded around Daniel, asking for him to look this way and that. He had warned his wife to keep back once these vultures descended before they realized he had a family. She didn't particularly like it but understood once she saw these paparazzi in action.

He was whisked off to a reception and then driven to a War Bond Rally in a nearby baseball stadium. They were serving BBQ Beef and had three steer roasting on spits. All of these had been donated by local ranchers. They threw him up on the stage and expected him to make a speech. He saw his family in the crowd and began, "Ladies and Gentlemen, I humbly come before you as a simple man who started his career in the Navy as a rating. I was a harbor pilot in Charleston who saw the unthinkable happen. German U-Boats were sinking ships headed for England for lend-lease. I couldn't stand by and watch that go on without doing something. So that very day, I joined up. I was inducted and sent off to gunnery school and served for two years on a Destroyer. During the attack on Pearl Harbor, I got to put all my training to use. We shot down several aircraft and fired up the boilers, got underway, and took out a mini-sub in the harbor. Then cleared it for the other ships to escape. Then we set up a cordon waiting for the third wave of attacks that never came. Then, a week later, my boat was raked with fire from enemy planes. All the officers perished, but before the last one passed, he promoted me to Warrant Officer with acting Captaincy. I was given the order to 'FIGHT THE SHIP!' and to get it and the crew to safety. I did that and was rewarded with a slot at Officer Candidacy School. Afterward, I was sent to Combat Training and Tactics and finally given command of a Patrol Craft, which we have been using to defend this great country from all enemies. Now I don't expect you to join up. But can I ask each of you to try and do your part? Whether it be to grow a victory garden, donate tin and scrap iron, or purchase war bonds. For if we have the tools, we can win this war. Thank you for your time." And with that, he left the stage.

The hype men were already starting in on him, "Why did you give the speech that way?"

"Why don't you write one and give it to me to learn and then deliver? You threw me on stage cold. That is what you get."

He then strode into the crowd to meet and greet and kiss some babies. He had learned how to pucker up. He didn't particularly like it. But he knew how to work a room and work the crowd he did. For several hours.

He got home around 16:00, went straight to the fridge, and got a cold beer. His wife gave him a slow clap, "Great speech. You are a regular Rhodes Scholar out there. Buy War Bonds? Really?"

"Sorry, hon, but I was voluntold to do it."

"By whom?'

"By whom. Well, let's see Franklin Delano Roosevelt and Nimitz. I was told that we needed an influx of capital to get the money necessary to make the bullets, munitions, and craft to be fabricated to win the war. Didn't you hear the President in that Fireside Chat? He said we needed a billion, billion dollars. How are we to get it? Buy War Bonds. We can't purchase the raw materials to manufacture what we need to win if we don't. It's a dog and pony show, and I wouldn't say I like it, but America needs a hero. They already have a dead one who won the Medal of Honor; he's out of the running, so they picked me—just a regular Joe who did well against impossible odds and survived. They will parade me around for a week to ten days, and then hopefully, my ship will be repaired, and I can get back to the business at hand. I'm sorry that it's cutting in on our family time, but it's just as necessary as everything else required of us. If you want to, you can come along. If not, I understand. But this is beyond us."

She ran towards him and hugged him, tears in her eyes.

Then they heard a scream that was cut off, followed by a hollow thunk and a crash. Daniel ran towards the bathroom, and the door was locked. He rapped on it concern in his voice, "Hailey? Are you all right?"

There was no answer, so he used his foot to kick it in. The doorjamb exploded, and it came off its hinges. He saw that Hailey had fallen in the shower and had grasped the curtain to steady herself and was entangled. There was blood running down her head as she had struck the tub's rim on the way down. He rushed to her side and lifted her gingerly. His wife and sister-in-law disengaged her body from the curtain and wrapped her in a robe. He lifted her and Kim-Yee told Miranda, "Call ahead to the hospital and tell them we are on our way with a concussion of a twelve-year-old female. Daniel rushed to the station wagon and laid her on the back seat. His wife hopped in with her Nurses Valise or "Battle Bag" and had her stethoscope out and was taking her pulse. He tied a white handkerchief to the antenna and peeled it out. Heading across the base to the main Hospital.

"Her pulse is thready, breathing is shallow," said Kim-Yee

"I smell a lot of blood back there."

"That's mostly from below."

"Below where?" he asked.

Kim-Yee rolled her eyes. "AYAH!"

"Oh. Isn't it a little early for that?

"But she has good nutrition and is much larger than I was at her age. She's due."

"Come on," he said as he worked his way through traffic, swerving to avoid a collision. They heard sirens behind him, and two jeeps pulled up, motioning for him to pull over. He shook his head and pointed to the white flag, then jerked his thumb to the rear seat where his wife was using a small penlight to try and get their daughter to respond. They nodded agreement, and one took up a forward position to clear the way, and the other brought up the rear in a phalanx maneuver. They pulled into the hospital's Emergency lane five minutes later, and the staff rushed out with a trundle bed and surgeons. They loaded her onto the hospital bed and raced her into the bowels of the building. Kim-Yee went with them, and Daniel opened the door. He was pulling out a pack of cigarettes and offering them to the MP's that had saved them precious moments to get here.

"Who is she?"

"The nurse is my wife, and the patient is my daughter. She fell in the shower and hit her head. One of the MP's shined a light on the pool of black blood on the seats and dripping down to the carpet.

"Ouch! I hope she's going to be okay.", he said in earnest.

"Thanks, fellas. Yeah, with your help, she probably will be."

The head MP motioned for them to leave and said thoughtfully, "It was our pleasure, sir. Take care."

They left, and he went and parked the car. Then, he bravely walked in to find his wife distraught and wringing her hands in frustration. She turned to him and buried her face in his chest, openly weeping.

"It's okay, hon. She's in good hands. I think we got her here in time."

"But she's my little girl."

"I know, and it will be all right. No matter what happens." The head Nurse came up to them with a clipboard and said, "I'm sorry, sir, but we need your daughter's information." He took it from her and nodded. They went to sit down while he started to fill out the form. His wife snatched it from his hands and angrily began to stab the paperwork in frustration.

He let her get it all out. All he could do was hug her close. After what seemed like an eternity, a doctor came to see them. He was all smiles. "Mr. Core?"

"Yes."

"Your daughter will be fine. She just passed out because she started her menses, and .... Are you going to be okay, sir?"

Daniel felt lightheaded and turned a little green. He crashed into the chair hard. His skin was pale and clammy.

"Nurse. Bring me some smelling salts, a paper bag, and a cup of coffee."

"Honey, are you okay?"

"What does he do for a living?"

"He runs a patrol boat and fights planes, cruisers, and subs."

"But mention a little blood, and he almost faints?"

"It's just the realization that his little girl is no longer a girl."

The smelling salts were applied under his nose, and he came back from blacking out. The cup of coffee was pressed into his hands, and he drank it in reflex. The hot, bitter beverage snapped him out of the grey vision that was overtaking him.

"I'm sorry, doc. What were you saying?" he said as the blood rushed back to his face, changing it from ghostly to a healthier shade.

"That you got her here in time, and she is now in good hands. We will keep her for observation, and you can both go home, or we can call you a cab if you like."

"I'll take the cab, please," Daniel said exhaustedly as he passed the keys to the doctor. Half an hour later, they exited the cab and slowly walked up the steps to their quaint little bungalow. Miranda was still up, and Jack had fallen asleep on the couch. He was dressed in his onesie that was too small. Daniel picked him up, took him to his room, and tucked him into bed. Miranda had some warm milk prepared, and he took a small cup and thanked her.

He drank the beverage and noticed that it was laced with sorghum molasses and a spoonful of whiskey. Once finished, he placed the cup and saucer in the sink and walked to the bathroom, where he took a hot shower and brushed his teeth. Then toweled off, went to the master bedroom, and fell exhaustedly into bed.

MOVERS AND SHAKERS
Pearl Harbor, Hawaii

He heard a hammering sound like a woodpecker, and he said tiredly, "GO AWAY!" The knocking resumed, and then he heard the screen door open. He shot up and grabbed his service pistol from the cigar box with one hand and draped the towel across his waist with the other. He exited the room and drew down on a civilian handler from the PR section. He could tell because the man had a PRESS badge in his hat.

His hands shot up, and he yelled, "PEACE! Put that away."

Daniel lowered it and told him, "GET OUT!"

The man hightailed it and retreated to the veranda but refused to leave. He called through the screen door and said, "MISTER. You are late! They sent me to fetch you because you are never late. So, there must be some emergency."

Daniel turned and went to the bedroom and started to don his clothing. He put the pistol back into the cigar box but not before removing the magazine and unloading the chamber."

"Yep. Had one last night. My daughter tripped in the shower and ended up in the Hospital. None of that is for publication! Compartmentalize it."

"Rodger that."

"We'll, call today off for divine services. Here is the new schedule for the week." He tucked it into the screen door.

"Get in here," Daniel said, sighing. "So, how much are you trying to sell these for?"

"What?"

"These war bonds."

"Series E bonds sell for $25-$1,000 at 75% of face value."

"What's the term and interest rate?"

"10 years and 2.9%"

"Well, people don't carry $18.50 on them. Do you have an incremental savings book?"

"What's that?"

"My grandfather told me that they issued stamps for a penny in the Great War, and you put those into savings books; when you had enough, you turned them in and bought the bonds."

"Smart idea. But we need to raise a million dollars this month."

"Looking at this schedule, you want me to meet with movers, shakers, and big wigs. But I think you need to insert the public here."

"Like what?"

"Like factory workers. They are running three shifts. So, let's make it a competition between shifts."

"I'm not following."

"Let's say there are 300 workers per shift, and they all bring in a penny a week or even donate ten cents a week from their paychecks. One to ten bonds a week are sold from a single factory. Then let's add the grocery stores, gas stations, social clubs, and ballparks. You can quickly achieve it, provided you can ramp up for scale. Plus, you can put stamp machines in gas stations, libraries, and diners. They can be set up in penny, nickel, dime, and quarter denominations."

"Can I use your phone to call this in?"

"Sure. Listen, the schedule is messed up because I don't have a single point of contact with y'all. So, from now on, you are it. If a decision is made, you tell me. Don't run it through the chain of command because that's where you messed up. You think it will trickle over to me. It won't. There is a war on, and if it's not necessary it will stop there."

"Whoa, wait a minute there, Chief. This is necessary. Because if we don't do this, you won't have the ammunition to fight it."

"I know that, and you know that. But the War Department doesn't care. It falls under the heading of ignoring. So once again. You coordinate directly with me. Okay, let's go."

"Where to?"

"The Hawaiian Civic Club meeting."

"But that started at 10:30."

"Yep, but they do the business first and then have guest speakers, so call it in and let them know we are on the way, and we can make it there in time for the brunch. By the way, what's your name?'

"It's David. Are you wearing that?"

"Yep."

"Why?"

"Because I'm home on leave, and I'm always stuck in a uniform. Not today. Just live with it."

"Okay."

They got into the Press Core car and drove 15 minutes to the meeting.

He asked them about the structure of their organization and what their core principles were.

The secretary stood and informed him, "Founded by Prince Kūhiō in 1918, the Hawaiian Civic Club movement is the oldest Native Hawaiian community-based advocacy movement. The Association of Hawaiian Civic Clubs is a not-for-profit organization that is a confederation of individual and autonomous Hawaiian Civic Clubs located across Hawaiʻi and the continental United States. Our clubs are organized into five councils: Moku o Keawe (Hawaiʻi Council), Nā Hono Aʻo Piʻilani (Maui Council), Ke One o Kākuhihewa (Oʻahu Council), Moku o Manokalanipō (Kauaʻi Council), and Nā Lei Makalapua (Mainland Council). We are governed by an 18-member volunteer Board of Directors and advocate for improved welfare of Native Hawaiians in culture, health, economic development, education, social welfare, and nationhood, and perpetuate and preserve the language, history, and music, dance, and other Native Hawaiian cultural traditions."

Daniel nodded in agreement and then started his speech. He wasn't much of a planner, just flew by the seat of his pants and this was no different. "That's all good; however, we now face a bigger, more immediate problem—the War. We didn't ask for it, but it is upon us. As community leaders, we need your help to get the word out about the need for war bonds. Just as you are helping your people advance through education and civic commitment, I am asking for help in your civic duties to the health, welfare, and safety of all people on these islands."

"We don't have many resources, so we must pool our money to achieve what little we have. We only have pennies to throw at the problem."

"Which is why we are going to have incremental passbooks. You can exchange those pennies for stamps, and when you have enough, you can make it a bond. If each council tried their best and could buy one bond a month, it would help. That's only $18.75 for one bond."

"The effort seems futile."

"So then let's talk business. If you invest in these bonds, they will return a 2.9% interest rate for ten years. You will be investing in the future, which aligns with your charter."

"We will have to think about it."

"That's fine, gentlemen. We will be in touch. Thank you for your time." As they left, David asked," Why did we go?"

"Our job is to give them the information and then let them decide what they want to do. I'm not here to press them, for Christ's sake. That's what the War Bond Rallies are for."

"But it was a total failure."

"Nope. Because look, here he comes."

David turned around and could see the local President of the Hawaiian council striding toward them with a purpose.

"Gentlemen. Wait up."

"Yes."

"We think it's a good idea, and you are right. Even one grain of rice can tip a scale. We will help in this endeavor. I've been authorized to present you with a check from all 18 branches for $337.50. Please make sure that you give us credit."

Daniel took the check and said, "Yes, sir. We will. Thank you."

David said, "See, we should have waited."

"Nope. We gave them time to think and thought only takes a second or two. By leaving the table, we made them come to a decision faster, as you just saw. They want to make the donation and get some press out of it. Take this down. The next time they want to give us a check, have a photographer on hand."

"Got it."

They looked at the schedule. "It says noon at the yacht club. So, let's be on our way," Daniel said.

"Who schedules a lunch directly after a brunch?"

"Don't ask me."

They drove over, and he gave a simple speech asking them to contribute to the war effort in any way possible. The old men of the club nodded and said nothing. So, he ate their food, drank the Mai Tais, and thanked them.

David said, "Well, that went over like a fart in church," as they were leaving."

"Not necessarily. When fishing, you can go through all the prep in the world, but if they won't take the bait, it doesn't matter. It would help if you offered them something that makes them want to jump in the boat. Like last time they chased after us; this time, they might not. People don't have disposable income that they can throw at a problem. They view this as the military's problem. Not theirs. They already have plans for their money, so you need to appeal to them to contribute in other ways."

"Like what?"

"Well, for businesses, it can be tax incentives or contracts. It can be more personal for people, like growing their vegetables in a victory garden or maybe a scrap metal drive. Have them dig through their attics and donate junk automobiles for the war effort. There are many ways to make money. These are just the ones that come to mind. Drop me by the house, and I'll be ready to go tomorrow. So, what else do you have cooked up to raise funds?"

"Let's see. I remember in your record that you had helped to sink a midget sub in December."

"Yeah, so."

"Well, that sub was dismantled and sent to the mainland where 22 viewing ports were cut into her hull, allowing the curious to view inside for $1.

"Everywhere she goes, she makes money. We can send her into a town of about 2000 and leave with $3200. What I need is something like that here. And you, sir, and going to be it."

He got back around 15:00 and could see through the screen door that Jack was down for a nap. Miranda was cooking. He took his shoes off and entered the kitchen. "What's cooking, Sis?"

"Char-Sui Bao, Chinese Broccoli, Seafood stir fry and Aubergines."

"Sounds delicious."

"Busy day?"

"Yep," he said as he sat down at the kitchen table and took a cup of hot tea that she handed him.

"Thanks."

He noticed a message had been left on the side table and went to pick it up. It was from Mr. Bettis about provisions for the trip.

"Hey, sis, I've got to run down to the bay. Somethings come up." He changed into his uniform in record time.

"Okay, bye then. Dinner will be ready at 18:00."

"Thanks," he said as he picked up his keys and left. He drove across the base down to the docks and went to slip 7. He drove right up to it and stopped. He could see the problem. There were way too many provisions, and the delivery people weren't taking no for an answer.

He strode up to Mr. Bettis and took control. "Hey there, I am the Captain of this vessel, and there seems to be some error as we don't have the cargo space to hold this many provisions. It looks like someone placed too many zeroes. Here's what we can do. We can take all the fresh produce and a third of the canned goods. The rest will have to either go back or be stored elsewhere."

The driver of the truck didn't seem to like that answer. But from the firm look, he knew the matter was settled.

"But what am I going to do? I can't go back with a load?"

"See the Harbor Master about the snafu. Your company has been paid, and the goods now belong to the Navy. He will direct you where to go."

Dejectedly, the driver climbed into the cab and left.

Mr. Bettis stammered, "I'm sorry, sir. He wouldn't listen to me."

"Let me guess. He took one look at your rank and asked to speak with someone in charge?"

"I don't know how things went off the rails."

He sighed and said, "Mr. Bettis. You oversee this ship. You are the de facto Captain. It would help if you stood up to him and those like him. This is a life lesson. When he asked to speak to someone in charge, you should have said firmly, 'That would be me!' If he still insulted you, then ask the master at arms to have him removed from the dock and banned from the premises."

"I'm sorry, sir!"

"Don't be. Just don't be bullied."

"Am I in any trouble?"

"No. If it persists, then maybe. But not today. So where do we stand on provisions?"

"As you can see, we have too much fresh produce."

"Get it below decks as fast as possible."

"We can't eat that much."

"No worries. We have another run coming up soon to Alaska, and I'm sure the men there would love to have a crack at fresh veggies."

"How do the bunkers look?"

"Fine and full to the brim."

"Make sure to get with the cooks and see if they need anything special, and the reefers are stocked appropriately. I don't want any steaks disappearing to the night rats. If I catch anyone doing it, they will be docked a month's pay, on principle."

"Will do."

"How are the repairs going?"

"On schedule."

"Make sure that we have replacement fiddle boards." These were boards hung from the ends of tables that prevented anything loose from falling off and crashing to the deck. These were especially useful on rough seas. "Oh, get some replacement records like 'In The Mood' or 'Jersey Bounce'. We also need to stock up the Ship's Store." This was a metal cabinet bolted to the starboard bulkhead in the mess hall. Men could buy sundry items like razor blades, shaving soap, candy, or cigarettes.

"Rodger that."

"Thanks for the cat. The kids love her."

"What did you name her?"

"They named her Mimi. Do you help with anything else? Shaving, waiting for that second ball to drop?" he asked dryly.

"No, sir. Thanks," reddening in embarrassment at the comment.

"Don't worry, lad. You'll get there." He then turned and climbed back into his car and returned home. When he drove up, he could see his wife waiting for him on the veranda with an unamused look on her face.

He smiled and said, "Hi honey, what's up?"

The glare got even meaner as she asked through clenched teeth, "Who is Mica Hyatt?"

"A friend of the family. Why?"

"Can you explain this?" she asked, holding out an envelope with a lipstick kiss and reeking of perfume.

"Yeah, that's her way of saying it's important and to open immediately. Go ahead and see what it says."

"Why? Isn't this private since it's from an old girlfriend?"

"She is not a girlfriend. She is a friend who happens to be a female."

She tore the envelope open with exaggerated venom.

"So, what does it say?"

She softly replied," It's an invitation to her wedding at the King Kamaya Maya Club."

"When is it?"

"In two days."

"See. I told you."

She seemed bewildered," I don't understand."

"Honey, I had a life before I met you, and I grew up with Mica and her friends. You will get to meet them at the wedding. I treat her like one of my sisters."

She nodded apologetically, "I'm sorry."

"Don't worry about it. I only have eyes for you. Oh, and the children. Let's go inside and have a nice dinner. Then I must make a phone call and rearrange a few things."

"Why are you dressed in your uniform? I thought you were on leave?"

"There was a minor snafu at the docks, and I had to iron it out."

"Don't you have people for that?"

"Yes, I do. A Mr. Bettis, who is very young and very junior. But I straightened it out in record time and could get back home for dinner."

He saw that Hailey was in a nightgown and had three stitches on the side of her right temple. She was moving slower than before and he asked her, "You okay there, sport?"

"Yeah, dad," she said tiredly as she sat down at the dinner table. It was a delectable green chicken curry that was very strong and very spicy. He noticed that they had watered Jack's down a bit. There was also a plate of spinach that had been blanched and then seasoned with oyster sauce, sesame oil, vegetable oil, and soy sauce. Then a plate of black Chinese mushrooms that had been desiccated and rehydrated and steamed.

They ate and caught up with the day's news. After he helped wash the dishes and the children were listening to the radio, he called David to check what the schedule would be like. David was chomping at the bit to get photos of Daniel at the wedding, but it was quashed immediately.

"Nope! I will be your trained monkey at places of your choosing. But this is private."

"Rodger that. But one can hope."

"Yes. You are correct."

He also saw that a care package from Charleston had been delivered and he placed it onto the table then called out excitedly to his family to come and view the contents. He was like a kid in a candy store as he unwrapped the plain brown parcel. Miranda brought a pair of scissors and he cut the box open. Inside was a treasure trove of treats. The first was a box of pralines. He had to explain to them that it was simply sugar-coated nuts. Then there was the saltwater taffy. The kids dove right into that. Miranda gingerly opened the box of pralines and tried one. She seemed to like it. Then there was the bag of sugared candies. Pineapple bits, yams, and mangoes. Kim-Yee opened that one up and bit into the yam and grinned in delight as the taste reminded her of home.

Next came the clear bags of seasoned rice as well as the seasoning packets with the creole flavors of Charleston. There was a big note from his mother. Welcoming his wife and children into the family, with recipe cards for all of the goods enclosed. There was a big bag of stone-ground grits and he just beamed in pleasure.

The next morning when Miranda woke up, she saw Daniel at the stove cooking biscuits with white gravy and sausage, plus the grits. "Good morning, sis. I thought I'd save you the trouble."

She just nodded and picked up the cup of tea that he had waiting for her. "Why are you cooking rice porridge with no meat?" she asked.

"It's not rice porridge, it's called Grits."

"What is a grit?"

"It's hominy corn cracked and ground," he said as he cracked eggs over the skillet and fried them up in a big batch.

Everyone drifted into the kitchen as the aromas were very enticing.

They sat down and tried the new breakfast items. Kim-Yee liked the creaminess of the grits. "How are you going to cook the rice dishes that your mom sent?"

"There are recipe cards included. It just depends on what we have available."

She looked down at the cards in bewilderment. "I don't even know how to pronounce these."

This one is called Jambalaya, the next one is Chicken Fricassee, then Shrimp Creole and Gumbo. To make the gumbo we will need okra, Jambalaya calls for tomatoes and celery.

After breakfast was over, he assembled all the ingredients one onion, one cup of celery and one cup of bell peppers all coarsely chopped. Then he cut up two cloves of garlic, minced them and began to show the ladies how to make the dishes. "For a Gumbo, we need to first make a roux, so to do that, we take the bacon grease and ladle it into the iron skillet until it melts, about three-quarters a cup. Then stir in a cup of sifted flour. Do this over low heat until it turns creamy. If there are any black flecks in it, then you have burned it and must start over. Gumbo is a stew made out of leftover vegetables and meat. You can choose to use lard or butter, if necessary, but I prefer bacon/sausage grease. Now we add the vegetables to the roux and mix in any leftover sausage and cook them gently until the celery and onions are clear. It's called sweating them. Now we take three quarts of water and some beef bouillon and bring that to a boil over medium heat. Once it boils, we add in the roux. Reduce heat to a simmer and mix in sugar, salt hot pepper sauce, bay leaves and Cajun seasonings, then add any stewed tomatoes or tomato sauce and let that simmer for an hour. After forty-five minutes, add in two teaspoons of gumbo file' powder."

"What is the file'?" asked Miranda.

"It's ground-up leaves."

"Like curry?"

"Yes. So now we melt two tablespoons of bacon grease in the skillet over medium heat and then add the okra and vinegar and cook for about fifteen minutes. Then remove okra with a slotted spoon and add to the simmering gumbo. Add in any extra cooked meat that you have on hand like the shrimp and Worcestershire Sauce and give it another forty-five minutes. Then right before serving add another two teaspoons of gumbo file and serve it in a bowl over white rice, and with some crunchy French bread.

"Now while that is all working it's time to work on the Jambalaya. We will use the same ingredients to make this dish and the difference between the two is that Jambalaya is a rice dish made with chicken and sausage. So first we start with the onion, celery, and bell pepper all cut up the same way and sauté them until they are soft. Next, we add uncooked rice, chicken stock, crushed tomatoes, Cajun seasoning, thyme, cayenne, and bay leaves. Then we give everything a good stir, cover and cook on low heat for 25-30 minutes. Check every five minutes to make sure it doesn't stick. Now we take the okra and meat and add them into the mixture and cook for five minutes or so. Then add salt and pepper to taste."

The ladies tried each dish and liked both. So, they sat down at the table and had a Creole brunch. The kids tried it, but Jack didn't like the look of gumbo calling it, "Dirt, but tasty." They all had quite a laugh about that and then cleaned up the kitchen and did the dishes.

MICA'S WEDDING

The day of the wedding arrived, and Daniel and Kim-Yee both showed up at the club in Navy Dress Uniforms. It was a simple building with stucco and a large lawn. They were greeted by a girl in a flowery style of local dress who placed a lei around their necks. The tables and chairs were set up with lots of floral arrangements everywhere. The tables were covered with white linen and crystal goblets. It was situated right near the royal surfing grounds and the breeze was magnificent. The view was breathtaking.

Mica rushed from around a corner planter and hugged Daniel with a familiarity that irked Kim-Yee. She looked absolutely radiant in a white wedding dress adorned with pearls. Always the gentleman, he introduced his wife, but all she could see was the red-headed beauty. Sensing her discomfort, Mica said she need to go to the ladies' room and rushed them into a bathroom. "Honey, what's wrong?" she asked in a charming southern drawl.

"You are just so beautiful. He told me you were a family friend, but it looks like much more."

"No, darling, you got it all wrong. We are just friends. There has never been anything between us. Even back in the day I noticed that he was always chatting up the head librarian, not interested in me in the slightest. She was a lovely lady, about thirty-five, but he was only seventeen. I saw how he looked at her and could tell he was smitten. But it would just be too scandalous. So, he and she never did anything about it. I could tell that they enjoyed each other's company. The question is, how much older are you than he?"

"Fifteen years."

"REALLY! Well, I'll be damned," she said, pulling out a small flask from her purse and taking a healthy swig. She offered it to Kim-Yee, who tried to refuse it but could tell it would be a faux pas. So, she took a slug as well.

"What is your secret?" Mica asked.

"I suck the life force from him while he sleeps." Kim-Yee grinned at her own joke.

"Sounds about right. I think we're going to get along just fine."

Then, like a whirlwind, they were back in front of Daniel, and Mica was gone. She met and greeted and thanked everyone for coming.

They went to their respective seats and the ceremony began. Kim-Yee remarked in a whisper to Daniel, "She is something."

"Yes. They broke the mold when they cooked her up. Her family is one of the first families in Charleston. They have money, and she would always end up with someone of means."

"What do you know about her betrothed?"

"Charlie? His family owns a bunch of knitting mills, and the war has helped with government contracts, so I think they are set."

The couple exchanged vows and then marched out of the hall to the reception. Kim-Yee saw that Mica and Charlie were working the crowd.

"Seems an awful lot like a business merger."

"It is. His family has a lot more money than hers and she has the class and social status for them to become even more successful."

Mica came by and grabbed Kim-Yee saying, "I'm gonna just steal her away for a bit."

Charlie and he were left at the table. "So, how's business?" Daniel asked.

"Fine. But I wish I were in your shoes."

"Really?"

"My dad had our business declared essential which made me ineligible for service."

"Trust me you're better off. I've fought in many engagements and there are things that I can't unsee."

"But people look at me with disdain, when their children are out there fighting."

"If they mention it, tell them you are serving in a business that is essential to the war effort. If that doesn't work, tell them to bugger off."

"I wish it were that simple."

"So, why did y'all choose to have the wedding here?"

"My Dad got it in his head that he wanted us to produce Sea Island Cotton and thought this might be a good place to start a plantation."

"What do you think about it?"

"The idea has merit. But I don't know the slightest thing about what makes Sea Island Cotton over regular cotton."

"It has to do with the salubrious breezes."

"Really?"

"Yep."

A waiter arrived with glasses of champaign, and they each took one, clinked glasses together, and drained them. "Let's mingle," Charlie said as they worked the room.

There were movers and shakers here, as well, and they remembered him from the War Bond speeches.

Meanwhile, Mica was introducing Kim-Yee to her bridesmaids. They were all gushing at how beautiful she was and remarking at how Daniel was quite the prize and they wished they could snag an officer. Mica just looked on with a conspiratorial look of glee.

Then the announcement was made that the Luau would be starting. All the guests went to their chairs and tables in the Halau Ho'okipa Pavilion that were assembled around an open fire pit where a pig was being roasted. It began with a torch lighting ceremony, then the hula girls were brought out in grass skirts and shaking their hips in choreographed movements that were quite sensual. He saw a few looks exchanged between the hula girls and several of the guests, and he knew that they would be seeing each other later.

The drums were pounding away and there were several other instruments in the mix like a ukulele and some sticks being smacked together, plus people banging away on a hollow log. It all worked together to create a different kind of music that he was not quite used to. He had been to Luaus before, but they were mostly casual gatherings at the beach around an open fire with Mai Tais and pork. This was more of the traditional affair.

As the show was being performed the waitresses brought out the food and there was a lot of it. Charlie looked at Daniel in a questing way to explain what was being placed in front of him.

"That one that looks like grits is called poi. It's made from pounded taro root," he said pointing to the coconut bowl that had a greyish mixture in it.

"Tastes like spackling."

"Moving on. This next one," he said pointing to a leaf wrapped around meat, "is called LauLau."

"What's the leaf?"

"It's Taro."

"Tastes pretty good."

"This next one is called Kalua."

"Looks like pig."

"Yep."

"What's this one that looks like tidbits?" Charlie asked, pointing to the bowl that had rice, pieces of raw fish and seaweed.

"It's called poke and it literally means, 'cut up pieces.' The last one should look familiar."

"Rice pudding?"

"Coconut pudding."

As the night wore on, they had a great time and after the ceremony was over, they went to the open bar for some whiskey. A few of the old gentlemen from the Yacht Club were there, and they grabbed Daniel and ushered him over to a table where they presented him with around $25,000 worth of checks for the war bond effort. He thanked each and every one of them for their support and pocketed the checks to give to David.

They said their goodbyes and took a cab back home.

TRAINED MONKEY

The next day he was back at it again. Meeting and greeting and kissing of babies. He was in a local hotel where they were doing a press junket, and a reporter asked Daniel, "So tell us, when are you going to write your memoirs?"

"I think that's a little presumptuous. Let me survive the war first. Then, after I'm thirty-five, we might see to that. Provided another war doesn't break out."

He had a photo shoot for Life magazine at the hotel, so he had to get dressed in a swimsuit. While he was getting changed, David approached him with a packet of cigarettes and asked him to smoke one for the camera.

"Nope!"

"Why not?"

"Because I don't smoke."

"But it will lend an air of sophistication about you."

"The answer is no. I will not do any advertising. I will sell your war bonds, and that is all."

"But this is part of that."

"NO! And that's final!"

"How am I supposed to sell the look if you won't cooperate?"

"We are here to sell war bonds. Not me. Just the bonds. By the way, here are the checks from those guys at the yacht club."

"There's almost $25,000 here."

"Yep. Now make sure that they get a mention in the local newspapers and send their bonds by messenger."

Charlie showed up and rescued him. "We gotta go."

"Where to?"

"A trip around the island to scout out places for the plantation."

"There will more than likely be nothing here on Oahu. You probably need to look on Kona."

"Okay so let's drive over there."

"Can't. We will either need to take a ferry or fly."

"Fine by me."

They went down to the pier and got on a ferry and coordinated a car on Kona to take them around.

The driver told them that were several abandoned local farms that were recently seized from Japanese. Charlie didn't like the implications of that, but it was a sign of the times.

They drove around and looked at several and then dropped by a commercial real estate office to get the contact information. Then back to the pier by five and retuned to Oahu.

He got back home a little late and there were pork chops and rice in the warmer. The children had been put to bed and Kim-Yee sat with him while he told her about his day. He was enjoying the last day with her because come sunup it was back to the war.

TRAVERSING
August 25, 1942

Several days out from Pearl the ship hit rough weather, and she started bucking like a bronco; up one wave they went and down another. "Attention, all hands! Prepare for rough seas. Batten down all hatches. Secure all watertight doors. Stow all nonessential gear."

They could hear the ship groaning and the metal stressing, and they endured it as best they could. The men had strung up hammocks and were riding out the storm grimly quiet. The meals were cold sandwiches and crackers. No time for anything else. But they refused to complain. They just got along and did their duty. He couldn't have asked for a better crew.

Finally, after two days of rough seas, they were through it and had time to survey the damage to the vessel. One of the gunwales was bucked, and the three-inch gun mount had primarily pulled away from the traces. They got to work on that immediately. They also checked out the "K" and "Y" guns and had done okay. The hedgehogs had some wiring ripped out, and they needed to put new eyelets in the ship for their safety and static lines. They needed to shore up the antennas and add more cables to secure anything that had shaken loose—just another few days at sea.

Then they were into Dutch Harbor, and a barge pulled up alongside, and they began to unload all of the fresh produce first. Then they got to work on the canned goods and anything else on the shopping list. He could see that the Cyclops had been run aground, and they were dismantling parts of it to repair the base. It had served them well and had come to a graceful end.

He was in his quarters reading letters from his family member spread out across the globe.

The first was from his sister. Theodosia.

Vmail: Hey brother,

I've gone and done it. I've signed up for the Civil Air Patrol. It took a bit to get myself certified as we have to pay a portion of our fuel for training. The hardest part was the dead reckoning that we needed to perform in order to show proficiency. And since I was working at the factory for a while, I had built up enough money to pay the fees. But now I have my pilot's license. I heard about women ferrying position for aircraft so I'm going to look into it.

All my love,

Thea

The next was from Ristarnt:

Vmail: Hey brother,

We've been on Canal Duty for a while and dealing with the heat that has been merciless. There are quite a few alligators here and the mosquitoes are relentless. The food's okay.

Tell mom I love her.

Ristarnt

MARU
September 10, 1942
Midwatch Aleutian Islands

Mr. Perkins was the Officer of the Day (OOD) under a bright moon on a rare flat sea when two explosions were suddenly witnessed. The ship went to General Quarters, and he anticipated a minefield ahead. "Helm, engines back one-third."

"Engines back one-third. Aye"

Daniel raced to the bridge. "I have the conn," he announced.

"Captain has the conn," said Mr. Perkins.

"What do were have here, Mr. Perkins?"

"I think we might be in a minefield, sir."

"What makes you say that?"

"Well, there were two explosions; the first was five hundred yards away and the other one hundred and fifty yards ahead."

"We were just patrolling the area yesterday."

A lookout yelled, "TORPEDO. Starboard-bow."

"Helm, Ahead, Full Speed," Daniel ordered as he scanned ahead with binoculars.

"Ahead, Full Speed, AYE!"

"Hard right!"

"Hard right. AYE, sir."

The second stream of bubbles from a torpedo swept past them, and as they completed the maneuver, the wake of a third torpedo crossed the bow, not a hundred yards ahead.

"All spotters find where they are coming from."

"AFT! Two surface targets," called a spotter.

"HARD ABOUT!"

"Hard about. AYE!"

"Fire all guns to the leeward side."

Shells from the 20mm and 40mm guns raked the Maru (Japanese torpedo boats) and exploded against their sides. They broke contact as smoke billowed from them and slipped away into the fog.

"Where are they?"

"They've disappeared into the fog bank, sir."

They heard shells scream overhead and listened to the drone of an airplane.

The TBS phone rang. Daniel answered. "Fire Illumination shells forward."

"Rodger. Gun mount one fire three illumination shells forward high altitude."

The order was relayed, and a few seconds later, the gun was firing.

Then more shells screamed overhead, and a fireball was visible through the fog. Then a bomb was dropped and another explosion.

"That got them," said the Captain of Destroyer Reliant. "Thanks." "Happy to assist!" replied Daniel.

"Reliant out!"

"Clear from general quarters but stay vigilant. They almost got us." "Now hear this! Clear from general quarters."

"Mr. Perkins, you are relieved. Go grab some chow."

"Aye, sir."

"And Mr. Perkins. Good job!"

"Thanks, sir," he said as he strode away to the officer's mess.

The next few hours were uneventful, and the action was recorded. Two hours later, Daniel was relieved and went to breakfast. It was corned beef hash with scrambled eggs, coffee, orange juice, and toast. Marmalade was available, but he disliked it. Today was Saturday, and they were steaming back to Dutch Harbor. They were scheduled to have Sunday off in port. He would sleep in and let Waisner handle divine services. He made sure to post that no work was to be done besides watches. He wanted them to relax. He would have Mr. Bettis ask around and see if anyone wanted to participate in a pickup baseball game, as he was the Morale Officer.

Daniel awoke feeling calm and at ease. He felt very rested and saw that he had slept for eight hours. He got up, donned his Greys, and started the task of mail censoring. He looked up at the saying he had placed above the wire rack:

■ ■

> "The Post Office, War, and Navy departments realize fully that frequent and rapid communication with parents, associates, and other loved ones strengthens fortitude, enlivens patriotism, makes loneliness endurable, and inspires to even greater devotion the men and women who are carrying on our fight far from home and friends."
>
> The 1942 Annual Report of the United States Postmaster General

■ ■

He started reading the letters, thinking to himself, 'Is this something my enemy could use against me if he found out?' His mail was also being censored. This was part of his duties and, in the beginning, seemed exciting but, after a time, got monotonous. He might turn this over to someone more junior.

The standards were to make sure that there was no mention of geographic location, what ships and types they were on, and the strength of their numbers. If any of these were broken, then he might heavily blot the area with ink or take scissors and cut out the offending remark. The same could be said for anything lewd or sexually explicit in context.

After doing that, he decided to read his letters and relax. The first one was from Hailey.

"Dear Dad,

Thanks for everything. Sorry I was a bother by falling in the tub. I told my father what happened, and he got weird about it. He kept asking me about you and what your intentions to me were. I'm not going to tell him anything more because it just upset him that you are in the picture. Anyway, just chugging on, and now I seem to get a lot of attention from boys. They keep asking me to dances, but Mom says not until I'm sixteen. Is that right? Am I going to have to wait that long? Jack sends his love, and the little stinker likes to play pranks. Auntie has a handyman come over to fix a few things, and I think they've got something going on. I'm glad for her as she is permanently stuck in the house.

With all my love

Hailey

The next one was from his wife:

Darling,

Hailey is blossoming into a fully-grown woman. She is getting very thick, and you were right about the boys like that.

Jack has been misbehaving lately, pulling pranks on everyone.

Miranda has a handyman come by since you are gone a lot on business. I think they are sweet about each other. But he seems to be a suitable type, and his prices are reasonable.

Love Kim-Yee

The next was a postcard from his son Jack.

Hi Poppa,

Gajje shows me how to write to you. Jack miss Poppa.

Come home soon.

Butterfly kisses.

Jack

He teared up at the letters and postcards, remembering that he was doing this for them. If he failed in his mission, it would cost too much overall.

He returned to reviewing his sailors' correspondence since it was less depressing. He noticed a trend that many of these men seemed to have a girl in every port, and they basically wrote one letter and just changed the names on them. They were smooth with their lines of bull. He just hoped that their antics didn't come with any fatal consequences.

He found some more family correspondence from his sister Thea. Vmail: Hey brother,

I got the job as a ferry pilot. I'm now in the Women's Auxiliary Ferrying Squadron. WAFS. We take the planes from the factories and deliver them to where they need to be. It's very exciting and frees up the men to go to the front lines. Can't say any more but I will be in touch.

All my love,

Thea

It was afternoon, and he decided to take the gig down to see the baseball game that Mr. Bettis had arranged. Airmen versus Seamen. On the way, he stopped by the side galley and used a key to open a small fruit box, where he retrieved a bag of mandarin oranges. He was pipped aboard the gig, and they quickly raced across the harbor to the pier, just a bunch of empty fuel barrels strung together with some planks lashed to them. As he walked through the sea of planks that they set up above the loamy mud, he noticed two men bathing in halved oil drums. Another group was by the ballfield eating their lunch since the mess hall was too small.

"What inning is it?" he asked as he arrived at the bleachers.

"Third."

"Who's winning?"

"The weather."

"Run that by me again."

"When they hit a pop fly, the wind grabs it and holds it, so the opposing team has a chance to get under it. Not fair conditions, but we're all having fun, so who cares? Right?"

He sat down on the bleachers and began to pass out the oranges to all takers. He told them to toss the peels back into the bag so the cooks could use them to make marmalade.

Thanos arrived by the fifth inning and asked him to come with. "Where are we going?"

"To meet up with Rear Admiral Thomas Kinkaid."

They hopped on a tractor carrying a flatbed behind it and used it to traverse the base as the place was just one big mud field.

When they arrived at the Command Quonset Hut, the meeting began. He introduced himself and told them all what they had mostly figured out.

"Gentlemen, we are entering into the final phase of this campaign. Those Japs are dug in like ticks on a dog. So, we will bomb and shell them into submission for the next three weeks. Then we are going to send the troops to mop up."

We have enough fuel to keep you all here for the duration. Try your best to stay ever vigilant and keep them from resupplying."

The meeting ended, and they all went back to their respective ships. He noticed a lone soldier on his knees tending to a small garden with a teaspoon on the way. It was right adjacent to his tent, and it was on a corner, and he had taken the care to use discarded lumber to shore the garden up and keep it above the tundra.

His brother Thanos flagged him down and told him he had some letters for him. So, Daniel followed him back to his Quonset hut, where all of the bomber pilots were housed. It was a typical setup with bunk beds, but these had been purpose-built on sight from fresh lumber and were stacked five high. He also noticed that the left side of the hut had pinup girls tacked to it from the floor to the ceiling.

"Wow, there must be over a thousand pictures here."

"You got that right."

They got to Thanos' bunk, and he went to the footlocker and retrieved the stack of mail. Daniel took the opportunity to place two oranges on top of the locker. "To keep the scurvy at bay," he said dryly.

Daniel handed Thanos a sports news magazine he had picked up in Pearl. They got caught up on family business, and he had to go.

He went back to the gig and, after a few minutes, was back in his quarters aboard the ship. He sat down, looked through the old newspaper that Thanos gave him, and turned to the sports section where they listed the pro and semi-pro baseball players who had joined up:

"Buddy Lewis of the Washington Senators is now stationed at the Armored Force Replacement Training Center, Fort Knox, Kentucky, leading his platoon's first squad.

Steve Peek pitched for the Yankees in 1941 and enlists in the Army at Utica, New York.

Boston Braves' second baseman Bama Rowell[1] is with Company C, 1st Chemical Warfare Service Training Battalion, Edgewood Arsenal, Maryland.

Lefthander Earl Johnson[2] of the Boston Red Sox is inducted into the Army.

Mickey Harris[3] of the Red Sox is now in the Canal Zone with the Army.

Dick Fowler of the Philadelphia Athletics, who lives in Toronto, has applied for enlistment with the Canadian Armed Forces.

Walter "Rabbit" Maranville is accepted into the Navy as an assistant to Lieutenant-Commander Gene Tunney.

---

1.   *https://www.baseballinwartime.com/player_biographies/rowell_bama.htm*

2.   *https://www.baseballinwartime.com/player_biographies/johnson_earl.htm*

3.   *https://www.baseballinwartime.com/player_biographies/harris_mickey.htm*

The first baseman with Madison of the Wisconsin State League, Hugh Gustafson, and a star defensive player on the Rhode Island Reds hockey team, is inducted into the Army. Gustafson was honored at Providence, Rhode Island before leaving."

There was also a local boy who makes good story.

"Lloyd Anthony "Frenchie" Rodgers was born on 16 May 1914 in Patterson, Louisiana. He worked in the timber and shrimping before working for Shell Oil. Lloyd was laid off from Shell in October of 1940, and listed in the U.S. Army Air Corps on 17 October 1940 at Jackson, Mississippi. Rodgers underwent basic training at Jefferson Barracks in St. Louis, Missouri, and was transferred to the 12th Bombardment Group, 82nd Squadron at McChord Field. He underwent Mechanics School at Rantoul, Illinois, and was assigned to the 12th Bomb Group, 89th Reconnaissance Squadron (later changed to 94th Squadron). Finally, he was assigned to the 434th Bombardment Squadron, where he is serving chief on North American B-25 Mitchell bombers. He served in this capacity from McChord Field, Washington to Esler Field, Louisiana."

CONDUCT UNBECOMING

After two weeks of monotonous patrols, they were ordered back to Pearl to make the best speed possible. When they arrived, he was told to depart the ship immediately on the Captain's gig. When he reached the harbormasters station, he was met by two large MP's who informed him that he was being detained "For Conduct Unbecoming an Officer."

"I'm sorry, what?"

"Just come with us, sir. They are waiting." He turned and shrugged at Waisner.

They placed him into a waiting car and sped off. Inside was a tiny man wearing spectacles and a Naval Uniform.

"Hi, there Captain. I'm your legal counsel. Bertram Russell"

"What's this about?"

"You don't know?"

"Nope."

"Well, that's good then. Points in your favor."

"Where are we going?"

"To the hearing. I'll let them explain."

"Fine," he said as he pulled his cap down and went to sleep.

Later the car stopped, and he was ushered out into a hangar. There was a long table of four Admirals, a court reporter, and other functionaries.

"Let the record show that all are in attendance for the charges of Conduct Unbecoming an Officer and Gentleman."

"I am allowed to face my accuser," Daniel said.

"So be it. Bring him in!" said Admiral Nimitz.

A door opened, and Gary Chung was brought in and brought forth.

"Place your hand upon the bible and swear that everything you say is the truth, the whole truth, and nothing but the truth, so help you, God."

"I swear."

"What is going on?" asked Daniel

"You are in big trouble, mister."

"What did I do?"

"You stole affection and married my wife!"

"Mr. Chung. She was your ex-wife for several years. I've even seen the paperwork," remarked Daniel.

"Don't matter. In China, we would still be considered married."

"Gentlemen. This is a total misunderstanding," Daniel said addressing the court.

"No! You've seen my daughter naked."

"Is this true?" asked Nimitz.

"No, sir. What he is referring to is when my daughter–"

"*My* daughter. You just stepdad."

"Still, she is also my daughter, legally. She slipped and fell in the shower and hit her head."

"Then you break down the door to see her naked body."

"No! I broke down the door to get to her because it was an emergency. There were two other witnesses, my wife and her sister."

"What exactly happened?" asked Nimitz.

"Like I was saying, she slipped in the shower, fell, hit her head, and was unconscious. By the time I broke down the door, she had tried to steady herself by grabbing onto the shower curtain, which was wrapped around her. I was focused on her head injury. I lifted her head and shoulders, and the ladies untangled her from the curtain and wrapped her in a bathrobe. We then called it in to the hospital and rushed her to the emergency room. We had an MP escort. So, as you can see, this is a misunderstanding."

"NO! I don't want you near my children."

"Why? What have I done to offend you? I have even gone so far as to deliver them to you for court-ordered visits."

"You steal affection."

"I don't know what that means to you as that term only pertains to adultery charges."

"I checked with the lawyer, and he said to say."

"Is that lawyer here?"

"No."

"As you can see, this is a lost-in-translation moment."

"I want to win," Mr. Chung declared. "How much does it cost to get the verdict I want?"

"Mr. Chung, that is not how this works," said Nimitz sternly.

"I am prepared to sell my restaurant to do it. Just name a figure."

"Gentlemen, this would be considered the normal course of business in China. His country has courts within courts. Whoever has the most money wins. Please excuse him."

"Mr. Chung, the accusations you have brought against this officer appear baseless, and you can be hit with punitive measures," thundered Nimitz.

"I see. This is how this works. The government lets him hide. Not justice."

Nimitz spoke up, "Mr. Chung. I will ask you questions to ascertain your actions regarding the children. Have you ever changed their diapers?"

"No. That's women's work."

"Pulled a tooth for them?"

"No."

"Walked the halls with them while they are sick?"

"What for?"

"Caught their vomit?"

"Never."

"Wiped their noses?"

"Why do you ask all this?"

"Because that man has done all the above, and he is still civil with you and trying to be understanding when you have slandered him and his good name. He is legally married to your ex-wife; the children are his heirs, and he is responsible for their wellbeing."

"But a divorced woman is not supposed to be worth anything!"

"Mr. Chung, do you have anything against Mr. Core, or would you do the same to any man she married?"

"I would do the same."

"Why?"

"Because when we divorced, she was supposed to be valueless and a beggar on the street. She should come crawling back to me and beg forgiveness."

"Well, it looks like she succeeded despite you!" said Daniel.

"Now the children call him dad and treat me like the stepdad. They even address me by my first name." whined Garry.

"Mr. Chung, all your complaints are based on your actions. He is their dad, and you are their father. Get used to it. We withdraw the charges and order the record to be expunged. Mr. Core, do you wish to bring a civil suit to Mr. Chung?"

"I do not. His interests were for the safety and well-being of the children, and I can't fault him for that."

"Mr. Chung, be warned that any further attempt by yourself to slander this officer will be met with the full force of the Federal Government. We stand adjourned, Case dismissed. Get him out of my sight, off the base and banned from returning."

Daniel stood as they exited the room. His lawyer turned to him and shook his hand. "See, I told you so."

"You could have warned me."

"No. I couldn't. We already checked into all his accusations and found them groundless, but we had to do this to keep him from taking a run at you in the future."

Nimitz came around the table and shook his hand, "Sorry about that, sport! It was the only way. We had to keep you off balance because that other person in the room was a shrink, and he was watching your body language, and if anything, Mr. Chung said were true, he would have pounced. He didn't because you are a good and better man than Chung."

"Right!"

"So, now I need you to return to your ship and let the rest of the crew rotate to liberty. You are going back out in a week back to Dutch Harbor. We need to keep the pressure up and the goods flowing."

"Rodger that!"

He was ushered back to the vehicle and returned to his ship. He used the ship-to-shore connection to tell his wife to come to meet him at the ship and that he would be here all week for replenishment and maintenance.

The next group of men left for liberty, and Kim-Yee arrived as they departed. He could tell that she was in a snit as she strode up the gangway with purpose. Waisner let her on board, and they went to the officer's mess.

"It didn't look that big at the docks and looks smaller now that we are here."

The steward brought her tea and coffee for him and made a big show of leaving and securing their privacy.

"What's going on?" Kim-Yee asked.

Daniel breathed an exhausted sigh. "Well, Gary had me brought up on charges as conduct unbecoming for alienation of affection."

"Isn't that for adultery?"

"Yes. He tried claiming that you were still his wife, even though the divorce papers are on file and permission from the government to be married and the children are my legal heirs. When that didn't work, he tried to make it about the children saying he didn't want me around them because I saw Hailey naked when she slipped and fell in the shower."

"But you didn't!"

"I know, and they realized that he was just reaching that point, so they shut him down hard."

"So, that was why those people interviewed the children?"

"Yes."

"Did he make much trouble for you career-wise?"

"No. He just made it worse when he tried to buy off the court."

"He didn't?"

"He did and got himself banned from the base as well."

She smirked, "Serves him right, and he's lucky they didn't go after him for wasting their time."

"How is everyone?"

"They miss you."

"Bring them around after 16:00, and we can have a picnic at the dock."

"I will. How much longer will you be away?"

"It's hard to determine. This conflict in Alaska is taking much longer than anyone anticipated. We have so much coastline to defend and can't seem to make a dent, and they keep getting resupplied. But even when that is over, it will go on to the next. I don't know if I can rotate back after this engagement."

"I know and understand. I'll make the children understand. Write back as often as you can. We will keep the letters coming."

She finished her tea and reached up and kissed him. Then, she grabbed her sweater and strode out of the mess and off the ship, never looking back.

Waisner came around a corner and said, "Wow! That's quite a lady you have there."

"Speaking of which, why are you still on board? Get home to your kith and kin. I can handle it from here. Release everyone who is not on report or a punishment detail. I want all well rested and ready for action when they return, as we might not get a chance to rotate back."

"Do you know something that I don't?"

"No. But it's just a feeling that this conflict at Dutch Harbor is ending, and we might get sent elsewhere in a hurry. Now run along. Go on, git!"

The children came around the next day, and Hailey was dejected. They had a picnic with Char-Siu Bao and hot tea. Kim-Yee took Jack and Miranda over to the dockside so he could talk to Hailey.

"What's wrong, Hailey?"

"I'm sorry, Dad. I didn't mean to get you into trouble with the Navy."

"You didn't, dear. The whole thing was just a misunderstanding of your father over what happened when you slipped and fell."

"He was carrying on like you were some pervert. He kept asking if you ever sneaked into my room late at night and kissed me."

"And what did you tell him?"

"Yes, on the cheek. Like any father does to his daughter."

"I'm sorry you got dragged into this, as well. It can't be easy."

"He's the one who's making it worse. Not you. Never you. I love you for being a great dad, and he's mad about it. Saying it's not right that she remarried. She should have never brought another man into the house. I told him she brought a husband into the home."

"I bet he didn't like that."

"No, he did not. I'm so mad at him for what he did because it's not right."

"Well, now you know what kind of a man he is and why your mom divorced him."

"Why didn't you both tell me about him sooner?"

"Because we didn't want to poison the well."

"I don't know what that means."

"It means we needed you to learn about your father through his actions. Not trying to sway you one way or the other. We wanted you and Jack to have as good a relationship with your father as possible."

"Well, he's destroyed that."

"That is of his own doing."

The rest of the family returned, and then they packed up the remains of the picnic and left. He returned to the ship and made the preparations for the next cruise.

Dutch Harbor Alaska
November 10, 1942, Dog Watch

They steamed into the harbor and took up their assigned position to guard the bay. Suddenly, a flare was launched, and general quarters were sounded.

"GENERAL QUARTERS!! GENERAL QUARTERS! This is not a drill; repeat, this is not a drill. All hands report to your battle stations. Lock down all watertight compartments and secure all loose items."

The Klaxons rang out with that "AWHHOZZAH!" sound.

"Mini-sub off the starboard bow!"

The guns on the shoreline were taking a bead on it, and they fired two hedgehogs overboard to shake it up a bit. It launched a bracket of about 24-36 mortar rounds fired from tubes off the side of the ship.

They leapt into the air and then fell into the sea. Once they touched something hard like metal, they exploded. The thin hull made the crew feel every single jolt of the explosions. But they carried on.

The 20mm lit up the night sky, and tracer fire erupted as the sub was bracketed and finally came up to the surface and got caught on the netting part of the bay's security ring.

A gig was launched from the shoreline with Marines onboard as they wanted to take prisoners. A whump and a heap of water were tossed into the sky. They could smell battery acid as the sub sank. Daniel had to admire the grit it took from the officer piloting it to take his own life and destroy the sub. There were two frogmen on the gunwales, and he could see both diving into the water to try and get into the sub if possible and recover any intelligence.

After an hour, a barge with a crane arrived, and the sub was lifted and loaded onto it, and it sped off into the night.

At sunrise they were sent out again on an anti-submarine patrol with a group of craft all designed to try and push the submarine into an ambush. They were charging ahead at full speed and banging away on their sonar. Every once in a while, they would drop a single depth charge overboard for good measure. He couldn't tell if it was working but the aircraft that they had covering them seemed to feel that they were on the right track.

He knew that the USS Finback and other subs were in the vicinity and looking for payback. The USS Finback had participated in several attacks on destroyers on July 5 and had helped to conduct reconnaissance around Kiska on July 11th. He hoped that whatever they were flushing their way would not be a problem for them anymore.

March 1, 1943
Dutch Harbor, Aleutian Islands

This was the big kickoff. The ships had been assembled, and the munitions had been stacked for weeks. Now they were in an all-out sprint to get this wrapped up. Still, the shelling and bombing in earnest took three weeks.

The Navy has shipped some brand-new fighters for the occasion: the Hellcat. Everyone was impressed as they roared over the bay and to the landing strip. He could feel the excitement in the air. They had been at this outpost for too long, and their equipment was getting tired. Now, these new fighters would give them the edge that they needed to win the war.

They were to escort a minesweeper over to Attu. They would have a Combat Air Patrol of the new Hellcats for part of the way. Halfway through the patrol they saw a glint of metal in the morning clouds and called it in. The fighters roared higher into the skies to engage the enemy. They used their binoculars to see the battle raging above them. One of the Hellcats broke formation and pursued the Zero. He came in from a steep attack angle at the nine o'clock position and fired his guns leading the enemy aircraft firing ahead of him. Letting those bullets meet the target at a point in space forward. The technique was perfect and the Zero slammed through the barrage of bullets and the gas tank exploded as the 50 caliber rounds tore through the aircraft.

Then, on March 23, the convoy set off for Attu. They had 11,000 troops, and halfway there, they encountered the Japanese Navy and set up fierce resistance. His job was to escort the troop carriers to safety in a lagoon and protect them while the Destroyers and Cruisers got to work. They were outnumbered but fought hard.

The battle raged on for several hours, and they had a ringside seat to the carnage. They were occasionally ordered to fire starburst shells into the air to illuminate enemy ships. They were at General Quarters for six hours.

Then, abruptly the fight stopped, with the enemy retreating into the fog. Both sides had taken a beating.

They sat tight until they could form up the convoy again and got underway. The expectation was the operation would only take a few days. Since their

Patrol Craft had a very shallow draft, they helped coordinate the landings and provide cover.

Once the troop transports pulled into the shallows and started unloading, sporadic fire came from the hills. The Gunner's mate took the opportunity to fire several shells in the general direction of the sniper. Suddenly, there was a hail of bullets hitting the ship. All guns returned fire.

"Christ, they are giving it to us," said Waisner as he crouched down from the flying bridge.

"Well, our job is to draw fire so the troops can land," Daniel replied.

"I know," he said as he kept flinching as the shots got closer and closer. Then a crash and boom were heard, followed by distant screaming up in the hills.

"What happened?" asked Daniel.

"The 3-inch fired a white phosphorus shell into the hills and nailed the bunker."

"Serves them right."

They kept a vigil as the troops continued to unload and charge ahead. They could hear constant fighting for several hours. Eventually the wounded were carted back to the beach, and the small boats took them back to the hospital ship.

He could hear reports over the radio as various pockets of resistance were encountered and dealt with. The soldiers were making many mistakes and paying for it with their lives. But that was war. Either learn really quickly or die. No two ways about it.

Once the last troops were deployed, they were ordered to patrol the area around the north quadrant of the island to inspect and provide support as needed.

After two days, they were ordered to escort the Hospital ship back to Dutch Harbor as she was full up with patients. The cruise back was nerve-wracking but uneventful.

Then headed over to the fuel ships and refilled their bunkers. Daniel got into the captain's gig and was ferried ashore to the Command Bunker. He filed his reports and was given the rotation of duties. The crew fell into a simple routine over the next few weeks. Fill up on supplies and cart them over to Attu. Cover all ships underway and protect those wounded.

They got back underway and rejoined the flotilla. They covered the men as they unloaded over the side from the troop carrier ships into the Higgins landing boats. They landed in a different area this time on the northern part of the island, unopposed primarily, but snipers were everywhere, and most of these troops had never seen action. The landing site was ominously named "Massacre Bay". The conditions were deplorable as there was snow, rain, and hurricane-like freezing winds.

There were also more injuries attributed to frostbite and disease than to death. They didn't have enough cold-weather gear. The Japanese had occupied Attu for over a year and had been acclimatized to the weather. The Americans had not. The troops kept pushing the Japanese further and further into the hills but the mud and cold winds that were hurricane strength sucked the energy out of everyone. The crew never complained and just kept up the grim work required.

Supplying the troops was also very dicey as the weather didn't make it easy. A lot of times they loaded the provisions, medical supplies and ammunition into the Higgins boats and watched them make a run for the shore. Then they would lower the gantry way and men would rush up to the boat through the rough surf to make a fire brigade line and begin passing the crates to the shore.

After several days more supply ships arrived, and they covered them while tractors and over a hundred howitzer cannons were loaded into the boats. Then they too were shipped to the beaches, and they set up shop and begin pounding away at the Japanese forces up in the hills. The beaches were awash in detritus from the invasion.

They could hear the radio reports as the bunkers were called in and the howitzers delivered their payloads and once blown up the troops advanced into the trenches. There was fierce hand-to-hand combat everywhere.

Daniel was on shift, and they heard the radio squawk. "Hawk to Slayer! Hawk to Slayer, come in Slayer!!"

"Slayer here, Hawk. What's up buttercup?"

"We've reached the ridge and are bracketing them in good. Be careful on your approach as there is a full moon tonight."

"Rodger, Hawk."

Then firing could be heard over the radio. It was at least eleven 30-caliber machine guns firing up in the hills. From their position in the bay, they could see tracer fire erupting from all points. The fireworks were beautiful as the main command bunker exploded.

"That got them."

"Moving on."

Then on the 29th of May as Daniel and company were patrolling their sector, they started noticing figures up in the hills charging forward, screaming. They called it in and started firing and they followed the charge, laying down as much covering fire as they could. They even launched ordinance like the hedgehogs at them. Hoping to break up the momentum as best they could. They were probably responsible for a few dozen casualties. But it would not be enough. It turns out that this was a final Banzai charge of over two thousand Japanese troops that had slammed into the lines and made it to the rear section. They could hear the ruckus down in the bay as both sides slammed into each other using anything that they could to club the other one to the ground. There were several hundred man-to-man engagements going on simultaneously.

Each group was locked into a deadly struggle. Some fired their weapons as fast as they could and then used the bayonet on the end to try and kill the opponent. Others used whatever was handy. Be it rock, knife, bayonet, rifle, entrenching tool, or ammo crate. The fighting was fierce and ferocious. One pair took turns shoving the other one's face into a puddle trying to drown them. The Japanese troops were far smaller in stature than their American Counterparts.

The defenders had never envisioned something of this magnitude. A majority of the Japanese were killed in the first few minutes of the charge, but such was the ferocity that they kept going until they slammed into the reach echelon guard. Who promptly picked up weapons and fought like madmen to keep them away from the howitzers that they were trying to take out. When the battle was over, not one Japanese soldier survived, and over a thousand Americans and Canadians were dead.

The island was searched over the next few days and there were a couple dozen Japanese prisoners taken. Most of them were badly wounded.

Daniel and his crew escorted the Hospital ship back to Dutch Harbor where they received further orders. Their next job was to escort troops over to

Amchitka Island to prep for the run-up to Kiska. It would take several more weeks before they would be ready for the next assault.

The troops unloaded on Amchitka which was only forty miles away from Kiska and set up their large conical tents in the rain and made camp. There was a supply barge off in the bay coordinating material, munitions, and rations.

They listened to orders being sent back and forth and arguments over which tents got full stoves and which got potbellied if any. There was not much to use for fuel except old packing crates, but they were mostly broken up and used as planking to traverse the muddy loamy soil.

Tractors were also brought ashore, and they started chewing up the soil to build a runway. Because of the soft soil and too much moisture, the Navy used preformed steel matting that was linked together to accommodate fighter aircraft. As soon as it was laid down a cargo plane landed and started delivering supplies. Over the next twelve days, a cross runway was built. They kept laying out perforated steel matting to accommodate a taxing area, standings for aircraft as well as accommodations for the staff and a machine shop, plus gasoline, drum storage areas, and bomb storage pits.

Special Message from Headquarters

HEADQUARTERS LANDING FORCE APO#726 NUMBER 6 D-A-I-L-Y B-U-L-L-E-T-I-N June 12, 1943 SECTION I – OFFICIAL E-X-T-R-A-C-T

■ ■

"I WISH TO OFFER MY PERSONAL THANKS AND CONGRATULATIONS TO YOU AND YOUR MEN FOR THE VICTORY THEY HAVE GIVEN US, AND FOR THE GREAT FIGHT THEY PUT UP UNDER VERY VERY DIFFICULT CONDITIONS OF HARDSHIP AND DANGER TO WIN FOR US A STRONGPOINT IN REACH OF JAPANESE HOME WATERS. THE ENGINEER OFFICER RESPONSIBLE FOR THE RAPID COMPLETION OF THE FIGHTER STRIP AT ALEXIA POINT AND HIS MEN ARE TO BE CONGRATULATED ON THE ENERGETIC MANNER IN WHICH THE STRIP WAS RUSHED TO COMPLETION AND MADE AVAILABLE FOR OUR FIGHTER PLANES"

"I AM CONVEYING MY SPLENDID TROOPS YOUR MESSAGE OF APPRECIATION FOR THEIR ACCOMPLISHMENT, YOUR MESSAGE HAS BEEN DELIVERED TO LT. COLONEL CARLIN H. WHITESELL..."

By command of Major General LANDRUM

August 15, 1943, Operation Cottage

The Zero hour had arrived, and the ships were ready. The troops embarked and Daniel and his men were escorting the troopships to Kiska. Thirty-five thousand troops were landed to an eerie quiet. They kept pushing inward from the lower portion of the island and the Canadians from the Northern end. There was a twenty-eight-man combined special forces unit consisting of American and Canadian troops. They were sent ashore at Gertrude Bay to blow up the main radio and radar installations. Daniel and his men were to sneak over and drop these men off in the bay quietly.

They did so in the pre-dawn light.

All of his men were at General Quarters and ready for anything. They kept their binoculars trained on the black boats that were heading for the safety of the cliffs. They would then scale them in order to sneak past the lines and rig the charges. They followed their progress and could hear fighting in the upper hills but there was no reaction from the facility. The men went from trench line to trench line and guard house to bunker, and either had quickly taken out the guards or were unopposed. After three nerve-wracking hours, radio silence was broken.

"Georgia Rain to Ice Dawn!"

Daniel's radio man answered, "Ice Dawn here!"

"Nobody's home."

"Say again?"

"Looks like they bugged out several weeks ago. No need to set off any fireworks. Call it in."

"Rodger that."

He looked up pensively at Daniel who nodded and said, "Relay that message!"

"But sir they sent it in the clear!"

"I know because no one is home. Send it."

The radioman nodded and started sending out the coded message to Dutch Harbor.

A few minutes later his TBS phone rang. Daniel answered it, "Yes Admiral Kincaid?"

"No sir. No opposition at the facility. Yes, sir. It looks like it's been abandoned for quite some time."

Daniel listened for a minute and then said, "Yes sir! We can hear firing up in the hills but not a soul is here. We are headed that way to pick them up. We will be ever vigilant."

When the commander came back aboard, he gave his after-action report to Daniel verbally. A scribe took it down, and it was radioed back to headquarters:

There were over a hundred Altus on the island. The team was supposed to find out what happened to them.

"The Japanese had used the topography of the land to shore up a rudimentary dam. This provided them with much-needed electricity. It appears that the locals were used as slave labor. The dam consists of railway ties and poured concrete over an earthwork. Water flows downhill through the force of gravity to the powerhouse. The intake ducts are sizable enough to accommodate a single man at a time. Once through there is the main observation deck with stairs leading to a catwalk overhead containing instruments. We did so and used it as a vantage point to survey the lay of the land. Nothing was moving.

The town consisted of a large communal building built into the earth with sod covering the high beams. A steel shed was erected that housed all of their sledding equipment. The invaders used this to store their bulldozers and crane equipment.

The villagers were not violent, but guard towers were erected anyway. Because they found a cache of hunting rifles. The records that were seized in the raid pointed to the Japanese freeing their brethren and repatriation back to Japan."

There was a lot of fog, many caves, and booby traps but no enemy. They found plenty of fortifications like dugout huts built into hills that were reminiscent of Aleut dwellings.

When they finally had an engagement, it was with their fellow soldiers, but they couldn't see each other, so there were a lot of friendly fire casualties.

Finally, on August 24, 1943, the island was declared secure. It turns out that the Japanese soldiers had retreated three weeks prior.

BACK AT PEARL

Finally, it was over. He and his men felt great. They had outlasted the enemy and knocked them off U.S. soil. Quite the Pyrrhic victory. He could return home with pride, knowing they had done everything asked. As a celebration he had the cooks prepare ham steaks and fried eggs for the men for breakfast. Lunch was Jambalaya with fresh baked French bread. The men dug into the fare with gusto. Some of them had never had the dish but they packed it away.

Daniel was in his cabin reflecting on the cost of this one naval campaign. He wasn't sure of exact numbers, but by his tally around fifteen-hundred were killed, several hundred aircraft were destroyed, over three thousand men were wounded, and the Navy had lost three warships and a dozen small craft. He might never know the full cost that the Japanese had paid. But he knew that it was a difference in orders of magnitude.

The crossing was uneventful and routine. When they arrived, Admiral Nimitz was piped aboard and said, "Mr. Core. You are out of Uniform."

Looking down at his Greys, he inspected them and said, "No, sir. I don't think I am."

"Well, I'm sure of I," he said as he removed a small black box from his pocket and opened it up to reveal the rank of Full Lt. The rank pins were removed, and the new ones inserted, and he was handed his new certificate of Rank.

He was elated at the confidence that Nimitz had shown in both him and his men. But he also knew that they were to be thrown back into the deep end in a couple of weeks.

He disembarked the ship and drove home as his arrival was unannounced.

His family was seated at the dinner table when he pulled up and Jack raced out the door and jumped into his arms. He tickled him and Jack squealed with laughter. He had grown some more, and Hailey's face had changed once again, becoming fuller. She now had more womanly curves, as well. He groaned at that knowing that he would never be able to keep her suitors at bay. Luckily, he arrived back home on her birthday.

She hugged him as well and Miranda was crying in happiness that he had returned home safe and sound.

"What's for dinner?" Daniel asked once the tears had stopped running down everyone's faces.

Kim-Yee responded, "Carnitas."

"Really?"

"Yes, sir. I got the recipe from... a friend," said Miranda half embarrassed.

"Well, it smells good," he said as he heaped the rice on the tortillas and added the carnitas, chopped onion, and diced cilantro.

They all chatted with him, describing what had happened while he was on his cruise.

Kim-Yee smiled at him as she was very grateful to have him back. But she also knew that it was short lived. He was career Navy, and she might end up losing him in the god-awful war. She chose to relish every opportunity that he had and would love him for the rest of her life, no matter what.

Bibliography

Report from the Aleutians 1943 Color Film, John Huston US Navy Patrol Craft, 1940-1945 (ibiblio.org)[1]

PC Patrol Craft of WWII: A History of the Ships and their Crews, WM.J.Veigle, Ph.D., USNR (Ret), Astral Publishing, 3rd Ed

Battle of the Aleutian Islands - HISTORY[2]

The Akutan Zero: How a Captured Japanese Fighter Plane Helped Win[3] World War II - HISTORY[4]

http://millercenter.org/president/fdroosevelt/speeches/speech-3328

Hawaiian Civic Organizations https://aohcc.org/

https:pearlharbor.org/the-fate-of-the-captured-midget-submarine-ha-19/

1942 Annual Report of the United States Postmaster General

Baseball in Wartime - Baseball in 1942[5]

A group of servicemen watch, and play in, a baseball game,[6] Mediterranean Theater (probably), 1942-44 | The Digital Collections of[7] the National WWII Museum: Oral Histories (ww2online.org)[8]

WWW.NPS.COM[9] ARTICLE 807th Battalion History, part 3: Attu and Misc. Alaska At War: https://youtu.be/HnP4RSzY7Bo[10]

---

1. http://www.ibiblio.org/hyperwar/USN/ships/ships-pg.html

2.   https://www.history.com/topics/world-war-ii/battle-of-the-aleutian-islands#section_1

3.   https://www.history.com/news/the-akutan-zero-how-a-captured-japanese-fighter-plane-helped-win-world-war-ii

4.   https://www.history.com/news/the-akutan-zero-how-a-captured-japanese-fighter-plane-helped-win-world-war-ii

5.   https://www.baseballinwartime.com/timeline/timeline_1942.htm?msclkid=302d5b1ec2ab11ecaef43ecb55221d1f

6.   https://www.ww2online.org/image/group-servicemen-watch-and-play-baseball-game-mediterranean-theater-probably-1942-44?msclkid=0382cc9bc41011ec95ff5561d26ecf9f

7.   https://www.ww2online.org/image/group-servicemen-watch-and-play-baseball-game-mediterranean-theater-probably-1942-44?msclkid=0382cc9bc41011ec95ff5561d26ecf9f

8.   https://www.ww2online.org/image/group-servicemen-watch-and-play-baseball-game-mediterranean-theater-probably-1942-44?msclkid=0382cc9bc41011ec95ff5561d26ecf9f

9.   http://www.nps.com/

10.   https://www.youtube.com/watch?v=HnP4RSzY7Bo&t=0s

Preview of Shining Through: War in the Pacific
Missing

Nimitz was in his office when the Yeoman arrived with Flash Traffic. He opened up the red folder with trepidation. In it was the news that PC- 234 was struck by a torpedo and lost with all hands.

The flotilla had fought the enemy for several hours and had managed to knock out two destroyers and one submarine. Plus downed over thirty enemy planes. They had done their job well by pulling at least one task force off the objective but had suffered heavy losses with a fifty percent casualty rate. He looked at the list and felt regret, but he knew that Daniel wasn't gone. He was missing.

Nimitz placed the documents in his drawer and locked it. Then, he went out to his car and told the driver to go to the hospital. He knew Kim-Yee would be getting off soon and wanted to tell Daniels's wife himself. They arrived, and he exited and sat down on the bench close to the main entrance. He hung his head as he struggled with what to say. He heard her approach, and her face turned white as she saw him slumped on the bench. As he rose, she shook her head; her voice cracked, "No! No!"

He strode towards her as she staggered, screaming into his shoulder with a wail of anguish. He hugged her and said, "His ship went down, and they are listed as missing."

"You sent him out there to die! When will it be enough?" she asked, her voice hard.

He pulled her back and looked her in the eyes his voice stern. "Every day I make decisions that cost thousands of men their lives. I sent him and his men into the fray because they are our best hope of winning this war. They are men of true grit! Our boy's not dead. Just unaccounted for. A lot is going on; it could be weeks before it all gets sorted out. If you get any mail from the Navy that is in a Manila envelope, don't open it. I will let you know when I know more," he said as he steered her to the car.

Ten minutes later, he dropped her off at her home. He was stone-faced as the car drove away.

"Thank you," she said, her voice barely a whisper.

She dabbed her eyes with a kerchief and turned around to see Miranda her elder sister and Hailey her thirteen year old daughter standing there. Both were barely holding back tears. She walked up the steps and collapsed into the wicker furniture. Miranda came forward, holding the dreaded envelope. Kim -Yee tiredly reached up and took it from her, tore it in half, and then threw it over her shoulder with disdain. Miranda didn't understand as she had already read the letter.

"He's not dead. Just missing!" Hailey started crying and threw herself into her mother's arms.

She held her tight and stroked her hair, rocking her back and forth, making shushing noises. "There, there, Hailey."

"Daddy's not coming back, is he?"

"No, my love. He's coming back, just not right away. There was a large battle in the Pacific, and your dad oversaw another group at Bakok Atoll. They did their jobs well but suffered a lot of damage. He should return next month."

"You promise?" she asked expectantly.

"I promise. Now get off to bed but brush your teeth first." Hailey groaned and walked off, acting like a martyr.

Miranda gave Kim-Yee a sharp look. "Why do you lie?"

"I didn't."

"But the letter said ..."

"I don't care what it said if you couldn't tell." She motioned to the pieces of letter blowing across the lawn.

"How could you do that? "

She rose and went to the kitchen and reached for the bottle of whiskey. She cracked it open, pulled a coffee cup off the cupboard, and filled it with two ounces. Opened the fridge and, pulled out a Coca-Cola, popped the top with the opener on the side. She angrily poured it into the cup and lifted it to the sky.

"Here's to you, my darling. Come home to me!" She drank the contents, weeping.

THE BEACH

Daniel awoke to feel weightless. His body ached, and he could feel the warm water, and the taste of salt and blood hit his mouth. A wave rolled him over, and he was choking on seawater.

He opened his eyes and felt the sand under him. Both hands had reflexively shot out, and he tried to get to his feet but couldn't seem to complete the motion. His ears were ringing, and he could feel the sun beating down. He staggered to the left, and his foot hit something.

It was a body.

He knelt in the surf and blearily tried to make out the features. But his eyes couldn't seem to focus. He felt around and determined that the man was long dead. He got into a position to do a fireman's drag on the corpse when he felt it tug back, and he fell into the surf. He then realized that this was a pilot still wearing his parachute. He undid the buckles and felt around for the knife at the shoulder. He used that to cut away at the risers, and he could free the body from the shroud. He also heard a large plop into the ocean, and his hand went under the water and came up with a pistol. But it was a break loader and not one he was familiar with. That's when it occurred to him that the pilot was Japanese.

He heard murmuring and saw two figures coming toward him. Then they were upon him, steadying him. There was a light slap across his cheek and an air of concern. His ears popped, and the water started draining from them. His eyes focused better, and he saw that it was Waisner and other ranks. He quit struggling with the body, and they each grabbed an arm and carried him off the beach to some shade nearby. He blacked out.

He awoke to the smell of a campfire and roasting fish sometime later. He was still groggy, and his throat was parched.

"Water?" he rasped.

A hand gently went behind his head and helped him forward. The liquid that hit his dry, sore throat was coconut milk. He greedily swallowed it until it was pulled away.

"That's enough. Don't want you to have too much and then throw it up," said Waisner.

He opened his eyes and saw that it was night; the stars were very bright, and Waisner's silhouette was bathed in a soft amber glow. He reached up and felt a rudimentary bandage, wincing as he felt a sharp pain. His head was swimming. Waisner was right. He did feel like he was going to throw up, but the smell of fish made his mouth water. He motioned to the fish, and a leaf was placed in his hand. It contained a piece of fish and a white disk. He mechanically fed himself while trying not to swoon too much. The flesh was warm and soft. The disk crunched, and he tasted rice.

"Where?"

Waisner replied, "From the pilot. He had a tin of these rice disks. Those must have been his emergency rations. We also got a medkit, some flares, and a pistol; he had a map and a codebook on him. Plus, this." He showed him a rising sun scarf and a picture of himself and his wife.

"Leave those with the body and ensure he's given a proper burial."

"But sir," another voice started to say, but he cut him off. "He was a fellow warrior. True, our enemy. But he deserves our respect as he fought well and has provided us with these survival items, including part of this meal. See to it."

"Yes, sir," said the voice, and several figures moved away from the fire to follow his orders.

"Sit-rep," he asked.

"Well, sir," Waisner replied, "Over sixty of us in various states of injury. Half from us and half from 453. We don't know how the battle went, but we saw them duking it out for several hours. What hit us? I don't know. But here we are at Bakok Atoll, I think."

"How are we fixed for defenses?"

"Just the pistol, flares, and a few knives. We've got some spears for fishing, and we've built a rudimentary shelter, but that's just a lean-to."

"See to something more permanent for the injured. Tomorrow have work parties make some weapons and have those injured that have use of their hands start weaving grass mats. Send five men to get more coconuts and any other fruit available. Send another party to find potable water and let them refill the coconuts with water. See if there are any reeds or cattails in the area as those top stalks can be roasted and taste like cornbread."

"Really?"

"Yep."

"How do you know that?"

"It was in the Boy Scout Handbook."

"Where?"

"In the Wilderness Survival Section."

"Good to know."

"I'm turning in."

"Yes, sir. Good night."

Don't miss out!

Visit the website below and you can sign up to receive emails whenever Donovan Corzo publishes a new book. There's no charge and no obligation.

https://books2read.com/r/B-A-ETGT-ELJBC

BOOKS 2 READ

Connecting independent readers to independent writers.

Did you love *Shine On: Invasion USA*? Then you should read *A Time to Shine* by Donovan Corzo!

Daniel Core, a gunner's mate from Charleston, SC, serves on a Two stack Destroyer in the Coral Sea just a week after the devastation of Pearl Harbor when they are attacked, and every officer is killed. He was battlefield promoted to acting Captain as a Warrant Officer by the last officer before dying of his wounds. Now he must fight the fire, the enemy, the elements, and the sea. Can he rise to the occasion and get the ship and crew to safety?

Also by Donovan Corzo

WW2 Patrol Craft
A Time to Shine
A Time to Shine
Shine On: Invasion USA

www.ingramcontent.com/pod-product-compliance
Lightning Source LLC
Chambersburg PA
CBHW031840170626
46807CB00004B/1554